Money Boy

Money Boy
Paul Yee

GROUNDWOOD BOOKS
HOUSE OF ANANSI PRESS
TORONTO   BERKELEY

The author gratefully acknowledges the financial assistance of the Canada Council for the Arts during the writing of this book.

Groundwood Books / House of Anansi Press
110 Spadina Avenue, Suite 801, Toronto, Ontario M5V 2K4
or c/o Publishers Group West
1700 Fourth Street, Berkeley, CA 94710

We acknowledge for their financial support of our publishing program the Canada Council for the Arts, the Government of Canada through the Canada Book Fund (CBF) and the Ontario Arts Council.

 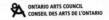

Library and Archives Canada Cataloguing in Publication
Yee, Paul
Money boy / Paul Yee.
ISBN 978-1-55498-094-9 (bound).—ISBN 978-1-55498-093-2 (pbk.)
I. Title.
PS8597.E3M65 2011   jC813'.54   C2011-902086-6

Cover photograph by W.Y. Park / Getty Images
Design by Michael Solomon

Groundwood Books is committed to protecting our natural environment. As part of our efforts, this book is printed on paper that contains 100% post-consumer recycled fibers, is acid-free and is processed chlorine-free.

Printed and bound in Canada

For Mohamed

One

English poetry crawls across our super-wide TV in easy words that I understand.

Hey!

I'll learn this ancient play from the movie version.

I'll get high marks on tomorrow's English quiz.

I'll surprise my teachers and my friends, who expect me to score another goose egg. I haven't read the play yet, not even in Chinese. That's how Mila Pei gets good grades. She reads everything in Chinese on the Internet as well as in English from our textbooks.

The movie starts. Men and women flirt at a picnic. One man is shirtless. The women's blouses hang low and wide below the neck. In the trees, birds are chirping. The actress reads more poetry, as slowly as before. She's talking about finding love!

Did our teacher finally pick a play that we immigrant

kids can understand?

The actors start talking. At first they speak slowly. Then they speed up. Rot! Mila chuckles at a joke. What was it? She chuckles again. This time Wei Zhang joins her. Those two are lucky. They had English-language tutors since primary school, back in China. Not me.

I lean forward to listen harder. I need to do well tomorrow. Otherwise my report card will cause trouble with Ba.

Mila's cellphone buzzes. She yawns and opens a text. She is sprawled over the sofa, feet on the coffee table. With a giggle, she thrusts her cell at Jenny Wang. Jenny's eyes widen.

"His clothes, where are they?" she squeals in Mandarin.

Scandal! It's Kevin, Mila's boyfriend. We rush to see.

"Personal!" Mila jumps up and grabs her cell. "Private! For my eyes only!"

She skips through the tangle of legs on the floor but Wei springs up and throws his arms around her. He reaches for the cell, squeezing her tightly. Mila screams and twists like a wild animal. Her blue hair sprays out like a shiny umbrella.

My theory is this. She wears her hair long in order to keep her shoulders and chest warm. Her tight tops always show lots of bare flesh. One look at Wei's face and you know that he's rolling in turned-on heaven.

The cell shoots from one end of our family room to the other. The guys hoot in surprise when Jenny catches it. Sprinting to the foot of the basement stairs, she shouts in triumph. Chubby Kai Ren tackles her to the carpet. Their arms and legs are windmills. His gym socks are blinding white.

Mila rushes to Jenny but my stepbrother Jian loops a long arm around her. They topple backwards, laughing. If Kevin saw this, he would crush Jian like a potato chip.

"Save me, Ray!" Jenny calls out to me. "Save me!" She curls up, tucking the cell to her chest.

I need to jump in. Otherwise I'll stick out like a maiden aunt at a wedding. I grab her wrists and pull her close. It's easy to play along. Touching and grabbing like this goes on all the time, right under our teachers' noses.

Jenny bites me. I press my lips to her cheeks and inhale her perfume. I hope to get aroused. Nothing.

"You vampire!" I hiss. "Want to drink my blood?"

"Give back my cell!" Mila hollers.

"Quiet!" Jian hisses suddenly. "Quiet down!"

He clicks the mute. The surround sound falls silent while the movie keeps going.

My father is at the foot of the stairs, scowling.

Rot. He shouldn't be home. On weekends, the restaurant is busy so he's needed there. That's why my friends came over. That, plus the fact that no one else owns a TV as super wide as ours.

At least he caught me wrestling Jenny like a horny young man.

My friends greet him as if they are at a funeral. Mila and Jenny adjust their tops. I straighten the sofa cushions. Ba always complains that my friends horse around too much and leave the house in a mess.

With his crew cut and bright red North Wind tracksuit, my father looks like he never left China, or the twentieth century. Ba sticks to Chinese labels. He says he's proud of China.

So then why did he quit the army? And the police force? He's still fit from those jobs, which makes my friends afraid of him.

Ba sucks in a breath. His eyes widen. I glance at the TV. My jaw drops. Naked soldiers laugh and toss each other into a giant outdoor tub, then splash and dunk each other. Inside the palace, women rush from bed to bed, undressing and dressing, pulling on skirts and blouses.

Isn't this supposed to be a serious play by Shakespeare?

"That," Ba thunders, jabbing a finger at the TV. "What is that?"

"English homework," Kai replies nervously. "We're reading a play by Sha-shi-bi-ya. It's called..."

He stops and looks around, but no one knows the play's name in Chinese.

"*Much Ado about Nothing*," he says in English.

"This play, it uses old-fashioned English," Wei adds, "so it's very hard to understand."

Jian clicks the remote to restart the sound. Luckily, all the actors are now fully dressed and talking and bowing formally to each other. And there's western classical music.

"Sha-shi-bi-ya is worth studying!" Ba declares. "He is one writer who is admired by both British and American people! But you should watch a high-quality version of his work, not this!"

This know-it-all kills me! My father never read a serious book in his life.

"This version is high-quality!" Mila retorts. "It was filmed in Italy. Look. The images are very sharp!"

"They are sharp due to my big screen!" Ba snorts.

My mind hears "you stupid egg" at the end of his sentence.

Ba grumbles all the time about kids who talk back to adults, girls who totter on high heels, guys who tint their hair, and teens who return to China because they are too lazy to learn English.

In other words, people like my friends.

"Stay for lunch!" Ba calls, blocking the stairway with

one hand. "Your homework, you can do it here. There is plenty of food, tasty dishes from the restaurant."

My friends politely shake their heads. They fish for their notepads and pens and load up their backpacks. Ba's bossy way, shouting as if people are army recruits, caused his fitness studio to fail two months ago. His clients were rich Chinese who wanted to be pampered.

"Look!" Ba hoists a shopping bag. "Special gift for my son, Jian-wen."

What? Usually Ba calls Jian "my wife's child."

My friends shout "Ooh" and "Wow" just from seeing the brand name on the box.

"Net-book!" Jian crows. The glossy silver case is smaller than a textbook.

My father isn't a generous man, so I know what's going on. Jian and I are both in grade eleven. Ba is pressing me about university and then medical school. His tactic is to surround and push from all directions.

He'll have to shove hard. I'm an average student. Below average. Very much below average.

"Many models are cheaper," Ba boasts. "But I want quality. Korean electronics are the world's best!"

Jian plugs in the power cord. Out chimes the Windows tune.

"My handbag is bigger than that!" Jenny laughs.

"The battery lasts eight hours," Ba brags. "None of

your westerner classmates has this model, is that not so?"

"Look at the keyboard," Wei adds. "Almost full-size."

Ba pulls out a camera.

Wow! The old fart made plans for this little event.

"Jian, show this to your father and grandparents," he says loudly. "They will be delighted."

This isn't about Jian's family. Ba will send the photo to my mother in China, to show Ma how hard he pushes his sons at school. He wants to prove that he is a better parent than her.

Ba tells my friends, "I told those two, if they passed summer school, I would reward them!"

"That was months ago," protests Jian, always the too-nice guy. "No need for this."

"I keep my word," Ba declares. "I am an honest man."

This honest man brags that he runs a restaurant, when in truth my stepmother Niang manages the front, the kitchen and the books.

Ba and Jian smile into the camera flash, holding the open net-book between them like a sports trophy.

I force myself to grin. I cross my arms and clench my fists to my armpits. If I storm out of the room, then my friends get caught in a petty family fight. If I stay, then my mouth must stay shut. If I show even the tiniest bit of envy or interest, I'll land in Ba's trap.

"You want a net-book?" he'll say. "Then study harder."

I failed summer school. Jian and I took the same course: Chem 11. At the start, I tried really hard. Then the weather got hot and humid. The school had no air-conditioning. The teacher spoke in a high-pitched voice. My brain melted. No matter how many times I read the textbook and the workbook, nothing made sense, not even when I found matching terms on a Chinese science website. Bonding this and displacement that — who cared?

Ba cared, and that made it a big problem. Chemistry is needed for medical school.

At the door, Mila gives me an extra-long hug and looks at my father from the corner of her eye.

"Nothing is the matter, right?" she whispers. Her thinking is this. Friends are more important than family because you choose your pals.

That sounds good in theory. But after four years, my best friends in China aren't so close, even with email to help us. Grandfather sends me handwritten letters regularly, and I send back hard copy, using Chinese software. He took care of me when I was in primary school and Ma the sales clerk hopped from one department store job to another.

Grandfather is nothing like Ba, even though they're father and son. Grandfather never asks about my marks at school. Instead, he writes about movie stars and TV award shows that he thinks I'm watching over here.

All of us have nagging parents, but I have it worse. Thanks to China's One Child Policy, I'm the only one with a brother who can make me look bad.

We're eighteen! We're adults! In China, by now we would have finished high school and moved away to live at college. But here we're a year or two behind everyone else because we were forced into ESL classes. And our parents still run our lives as if we are six-year-olds.

Steel has killed many men. Now he's a traitor to Central after leading several of its armies into battle. In a surprise turn, he defected to the Eastern rebels.

Rebel State takes place in China, so I know the landscape from my middle-school geography. The rivers and mountains that protect the rebels are as real as home to me, just like today's cities of tall buildings and traffic jams.

Central sent armies by land and sea against us. Yesterday, when its navy attacked, we catapulted fireballs from the shore and forced them to retreat.

Now smaller teams will get closer to their ships. I (Steel, that is) choose Long Range the archer and Monkey, the lightest warrior in my team, for this mission. Many teams wait for the Go signal.

"Where are you?" Ba yells.

Old fart! Nothing should ever make him wait, certainly nothing as useless as my on-line role-play games.

"Just a minute!"

Uncle Bei arrived half an hour ago. Grandfather is supposed to come from China for a visit. Ba sent him airfare long ago, but Grandfather keeps delaying the trip. He is terrified of stepping onto an airplane. Toronto has more snow and ice than Beijing, so Ba is building a small bandstand in the backyard. Grandfather can do his daily tai-chi routines there, under a roof.

The project has fallen behind schedule. Ba needs to finish it before the cold weather hits.

My bedroom door pops open.

"Didn't I tell you to quit that game?" Ba shouts. "Rotting waste of time!"

Messages from Rebel Command are coming in swift and thick.

Ba grabs the power cord. "Want me to yank this?"

I jump up, hands and palms up in surrender. Before I can even log off, Ba drags me to the backyard.

I curse to myself. It wasn't easy for Rebel Command to find a time when all the teams could join in. If I don't show up, my Honor will drop.

In the drawings, the bandstand looks like a Chinese-style pavilion. So far it's a birthday-cake frame of eight posts.

But how did Ba manage to pour the concrete and get each post to stand straight? He never built anything in his life. He barreled ahead claiming that D-I-Y was the Canadian way. D-I-Y means do-it-yourself, he bragged.

Too bad Grandfather won't use the bandstand. He says tai-chi must be done in the open air where nature's energy flows freely. All this is a big waste of time.

When I was small and we visited Grandfather, Ba barely spoke to him. If they talked, they cursed and argued. We left as soon as the meal ended. Then Ba brooded at home in front of the TV with a bottle of liquor. Grandfather didn't drink, and nobody drank in front of him. But Ma needed him to get me to primary school and back, so we visited. I always felt safe with him. It was his idea to start me in gymnastics while my bones were still soft.

Uncle Bei climbs the ladder as Ba ties rope to a long aluminum scaffold. My head screams at him to hurry.

Uncle Bei and Ba met in the army and brawled their way through China, getting drunk at every chance, if you believe their tales. They "served the people," while the people served them beer. Uncle Bei introduced his sister to Ba, a meeting that sent our families sliding downhill toward two divorces.

"That goes on top." Ba points at the scaffold.

"The posts are strong enough?" I ask.

"Today we will finish the roof." He points to a stack of wooden beams, neatly sorted by length and width.

It could take all afternoon!

Ba and I raise one end of the scaffolding to Uncle Bei.

"Push!" Ba shouts. "Not so fast! Pull it back!"

Bit by bit, we thrust the walkway up. Uncle Bei pulls it over a top beam. Ba climbs the other ladder across from Uncle Bei. They slide the scaffold into the middle. Then they come down to read the instructions. Ba has laid out his tools on the bench as tidily as trinkets at an outdoor market. Too bad he doesn't know what half the tools are for.

I head to the house but Ba calls, "Not finished yet!"

I don't always obey Ba, but I never defy him in front of other adults. Nothing makes him madder than losing face, even before family like Uncle Bei.

I wait.

In our neighborhood, people build high fences, so each backyard is private. There, they do whatever they want: tan their bodies into tree bark, barbecue entire goats, or let their dogs use the yard as an outdoor toilet. Some people grow flowers, while others put up playground sets. It's not like the front, where no fences mar the long slope of lawn. Everyone competes to grow the softest, greenest grass. All this is a farting headache of extra work because I have to cut the lawn and set out the sprinkler. In China, we never paid attention to the outside of our building.

This house is still Ba's new toy, even after we've lived here for two years. Our first two years in Canada were spent in a condo, so Ba came late to house care. He still asks the Chinese radio station for handyman advice. Should the air-conditioner be covered in the winter? How high should lawn grass grow? Can he remove black smudges from a white-painted wall?

I hear a sharp creak and a rasping cracking sound.

Uh-oh. Two bandstand posts are tilting, bending at the foundation. Other posts stay firmly planted. The frame breaks apart in pieces. Looks like the scaffold was too heavy.

Ba runs forward but Uncle Bei shouts, "Back off! Want to die?"

With a dull thud, the scaffold crashes to the ground, along with half of the upper frame.

"I told you, but you didn't listen!" Uncle Bei laughs so hard that his teeth are going to fly out. "You measured wrong for your batch of concrete. Look at my posts! Nothing wrong with them!"

"You should have stopped me!" Ba mutters. "This is blood-and-sweat money wasted."

Ba's face falls apart from disbelief. It's not a look I see often. My father thinks he is close to perfection.

This collapse will enrage him, coming so soon after the failure of his fitness studio. Good.

A car door slams in the driveway. Niang has come home to shower and change from slacks into a dress for the evening. She enters the backyard.

Uncle Bei dances over, laughing all the while.

"Look at that dumb melon husband of yours," he gloats. "I told him to follow me in mixing the concrete, but he didn't listen."

If Niang starts to chuckle, I may join in. Ba will be humiliated. She told him several times to hire real carpenters. She doubted that his English was good enough to read the instructions.

Niang walks around the wrecked bandstand. She tugs at the standing posts, testing their strength.

I am edging away when she says to Ba, "What are you waiting for? We need to move the metal off the wood."

She hollers for me, and I move quickly. I never give her any reason to scold me. Niang gets things done quickly, which is good for a house of lazy guys. As a teenager, she trekked alone into the city to look for wage work. After several hungry days, she started washing dishes in the laneway behind a restaurant. Then she learned the business by watching.

"Your daughter, Yan, brought friends to the restaurant," she tells Uncle Bei.

Together, the four of us lift the aluminum off the wood. No one knows which way we should go.

"I told them not to pay," Niang continues, "but they wouldn't listen. They left a stack of cash behind."

"Stupid girl," Uncle Bei grunts. "You should remind her that she's spending my money."

"She needs foreigner friends."

"She'll make them at university."

"She should broaden her circle now."

Ba orders us to lean the scaffold against the fence in order to prevent damage to his precious lawn. Head down, he trudges inside.

"I have to make a phone call," he mumbles.

He's trying to save face, that's all.

"Good thing you're not building the Beijing Stadium," Uncle Bei calls. "Otherwise our Olympic Games would have been cancelled this year!"

I get back to the raid just in time. Monkey and Long Range are angry.

Shit Egg, you will regret jerking us around.

You Dog Fart, go play elsewhere if you can't be on time.

No time to explain. Long Range and I are stronger, so we row the skiff. The sea is calm. It's so dark that the enemy can't see us, nor can we see them. We almost crash into the warships.

The signal comes, Monkey strikes the flint, and Long

Range shoots flaming arrows at the ships.

We hear loud splashes and then our retreat signal. Enemy Water Warriors are coming!

We're rowing as fast as we can when a dark figure swings aboard our skiff. I charge forward with my sword. He twists to the side. We both sway.

Long Range has one last arrow, but she can't see in the dark. If she shoots blindly, then there's a fifty-fifty chance that she'll kill me. And Monkey is too far away to help.

Two

Next day, I rush home after school. Music and graphics are sharper and clearer on the desktop, so I'd rather play my games there.

This morning, Central's navy sailed into our harbor, using two damaged ships as shields against our fireballs. One ship was the one my team attacked yesterday. We should have sunk it by diving underwater and drilling into it. But once Long Range shot the Water Warrior, we raced back to the shore. Then Rebel Command raised a Red Flag, calling its teams to a beachhead battle this afternoon. It's a good time for me to build up my Honor.

Wei is taking his mother to the doctor, so he drives me home. He loves cruising in his father's new BMW but grumbles about being away from the gang. This afternoon they're going to the mall. I complain about the

English exam, which was a disaster for me. Wei doesn't reply, so he must have done okay.

I want my driver's license, too, but Ba won't pay for the course until my grades improve. I hate how everything in my life is tied to school.

While my ancient computer grunts slowly through boot-up, I visit Ba's muscle machine. There's just enough time for two sets of bench presses, chest flies and pullovers. In my head I hear the gym teacher shouting, "Go slow for bulk!" but my counting speeds up as soon as I think of the upcoming battle. At the mirror, I flex my chest. My body looks more and more like Steel's.

Logging onto *Rebel State*, I sense someone watching me. My head jerks up. The house should be empty.

Ba is at the door holding a sheaf of papers and staring at me. His gaze is still and intense. The desktop screen is reflected in his eyes. I wait for his lecture to start. No doubt it'll be the same one about wasting time on this game.

"You're home early," I say, breaking the deadly silence. If I had known he was home, I would have gone to the Milky Way Café to play in peace on my laptop. At this time of the day, Ba usually goes to Uncle Bei's computer store in the Great Lakes Mall. He says he needs a break from the restaurant.

He drops sheets of computer printout onto my keyboard. Each page contains lines that are highlighted with a marker.

A chill cuts through me. The list shows all the websites I visited in the past two weeks. *Rebel State* appears the most. But the sites that stand out in bright green are all the gay Chinese ones — some in North America, some in Taiwan and Hong Kong.

"Why are you snooping through my computer?" I demand. "Privacy is protected in this country, don't you know?"

"Those sites, did you visit them?" he barks.

Why does he bother to ask? His snoop program gives him plenty of proof. I'm not stupid enough to accuse a computer of making mistakes.

"I was doing research for a school project."

"Show me the document. Which class was it for?"

"Maybe I didn't save a copy on this machine." I try to sound annoyed. "I can't remember."

"Is it on your laptop?" Ba demands.

I scroll through my desktop as my brain begs some faraway god for a miracle.

Take Ba away, I pray, and I'll quit the game forever. I won't waste another penny on this evil habit!

My throat tightens and my stomach clenches.

I want to scream out, I haven't done anything! I want

a girlfriend. I want to get drunk with my buddies, sing karaoke all night long. All I want is a normal life, passing one day at a time. I don't want my friends backing away from me in the shower room or in a row of seats at the theater.

Here's the file full of gay stuff from the net. Delete, delete, delete.

All the websites say that it's best if you choose the time and place to talk to people about gay topics, especially your parents. *Every family is different, so only you will know the ideal time. Plan carefully.*

Too bad there's no such time for a father who has actually killed people in the line of duty. In the army, Ba was in charge of training new recruits. His specialty was hand-to-hand combat. Only drunken fools who had lost all their worldly sense dared to challenge him.

He and I are the same height now. I'm still strong from gymnastics, even though I quit during middle school. But Ba is the one who knows how to fight.

"You know, all my life, I behaved well," Ba says quietly. "It is important that people respect you."

Here comes the standard lecture about proper behavior. Serve the people. Strengthen yourself. Stand tall. Don't wait until the cooked duck has flown. He complains that we young people have no idea how terribly the Chinese people suffered in earlier times.

"I quit school at age fourteen to help your grandfather," he starts. "Farmers were finally allowed to sell produce on the free market. Everyone rushed to grow crops."

He turns to my chest of drawers and pulls out the top one. He dumps my socks and underwear onto the floor and flings the drawer aside.

Hey! Niang just did the laundry yesterday. Who's cleaning this up? Not me!

"Farm life was wretched. Your grandfather forced me to join the army, did you know that?"

Ba empties more drawers. I sniff the air. Is he drunk?

"He wanted his son to become a four-star general," Ba declares sourly. "I served ten years. Then I got discharged. Your grandfather blamed me, called me stupid. He said that so many countries planned to attack China, its leaders would never dare shrink its army!"

I've heard this before, whenever Ba drinks. I never saw Ba show respect to Grandfather, not at family gatherings, not at New Year's. To be called stupid by Grandfather, was that enough to make Ba angry all his life?

Ba walks into my closet, bigger than our living room back in China. He dumps my clothes onto the carpet.

"Ba!" I shout. "What are you doing?"

"Then I joined the police force," he says, sighing. He scoops up an armful of my clothes and strolls away.

By the time I reach the front door, my fashion choices are front-page news on the lawn.

Luckily, I live by a labels-only motto. Every piece of underwear bears a high-end logo, in case anyone is looking. I run down to grab my jockstrap, even though Ba's doing a great job of shaming our family all by himself.

It dawns on me that Ba is throwing me out. This is serious!

Can he do that?

Of course he can.

The autumn was dry, and tattered red and yellow leaves lie everywhere. Across the street, Mrs. Lo is raking her lawn and averting her eyes.

Ba has gone crazy. You don't throw your son out of the house just because he visited a few controversial websites.

Do you?

I run around the pile of clothes, rescuing items. It took me ages to find the perfect graphics on my T-shirts. My gray hoodie is just two weeks old. Which should I grab, old jeans or newer ones? What about my combats? Jenny liked how mine were different from everyone else's. I can wear plain white T-shirts with anything.

Good thing the westerner people live too far down the street to watch us shame ourselves in public. They are friendly enough, always waving and smiling so that no one can accuse them of racism. We take great care never to step on their lawns, and never to park in front of their houses. We must never give them reason to complain about immigrants or to look down at us.

Ba hurries by with my backpacks and gym bags, and then shakes out my shoes. This must give him great pleasure. He has long grumbled about the steep prices of sneakers and how we own far too many pairs.

The red ones are for basketball. I wear the white Nikes for gym class. The black high-tops are good for slave labor at the restaurant. And I wear my Jordans when the gang plans a day at the mall or goes to a movie. I should have thrown out the other pairs long ago, but they're old friends.

Is Ba going to toss gasoline over them and click his lighter? He might be crazy enough.

I dash into the house for my laptop. Should I grab my CDs? I told myself to load them onto my iPod long ago. Now it's too late.

Ba puts an arm around me and walks me toward the front door.

"Canada was to be a new start," he says, "but how many failed businesses have I had? Four. One for each year — "

"Ba, wait! Let's talk!"

"Now you want to be gay. What should I think?" he says. "Your grandfather was right. I am a failure. I should have used more discipline to raise you. Now it is too late. Get going."

He pushes me out the front door as if he's escorting a drunken customer from the restaurant.

I'm speechless. I'm waiting for him to lose his temper and storm around like he does after parent-teacher meetings. Those times, he hurls dishes to the floor and shatters them. He threatens to cut off high-speed Internet at home, crush my cellphone or put locks on my computer. He shouts until he thinks he has scared me into obeying him.

But what do I do when Ba acts like this?

He shuts the door firmly. The lock clicks into place and the chain rattles. The radio station said we needed industrial-strength locks and a steel-plated door to be safe.

Rot him!

I kick the pile of clothes and one blue Converse flies next door.

I haven't done anything!

In China, he bragged about how wonderful Canada was, and how we would enjoy great freedom here.

Hah! He never meant for me to enjoy living here.

He told his friends that immigration was stressful and required hard work, but said he would sacrifice everything for my sake. He wanted me to have more choices than were available in China.

This is all his fault. If he hadn't forced me to come to Canada, I would never have logged onto those sites. They're not available in China. Even if they were, I wouldn't risk getting China's Internet police on my back.

Two westerner boys stop on the sidewalk. They sit back on their bicycles, eyeing me as if I am a toddler with a dripping diaper. They are in junior middle school. One runs a hand through his long brown hair and then shakes it loose. He says something that ends with, "...yard sale?"

"Get the hell out of here!" I bark.

Startled, they leave right away. I don't care if the fart-baskets tell their parents that I swore at them.

I grab some clothes and jam them into a backpack. At the last minute, I take socks and underwear. I zip up my down jacket. Winter isn't here yet, but I feel chilled.

"No trouble, is there?" asks Mrs. Lo.

I almost jump. She crossed the street quietly, carrying Ching-ching, the white puffball that is supposed to be a dog.

Ching-ching wriggles in Mrs. Lo's arms, blinking its big brown eyes and batting its paws at me. Mrs. Lo holds it up, and the dog licks my face.

My face crumples.

I back off and take a deep breath.

"Oh, no." I answer her question cheerfully and scratch the dog's ears. "No trouble. No trouble at all."

It's impossible to be rude to her. She moves slowly and gracefully, exactly like my popo in China. She even wears the same half-black, half-transparent eyeglass frames as my grandmother.

"Want to come over and sit for a while?" she asks.

I open my mouth but all that comes out is a strangled croak. I shake my head and shove the rest of the clothes beside the stairs, out of sight.

I'm being kicked out of home by an insane father, yet I'm trying to make sure our house looks good. Go figure.

Three

When I step onto the bus, I reach for my iPod.

Rot! It's not on me. It's in the other backpack with my school stuff.

I jam my computer buds into my ears but don't connect them. I need to save my battery. Walking around without wires looks pitiful, and even sadder if you're alone.

You look like you don't know music. You look poor.

Ba wants to humiliate me. That's why he kicked me out. He wants me crawling back to him so that he can control my life one hundred percent.

Every time the bus stops, I turn to the window to avoid seeing any familiar faces. I want to smash my fist into the glass.

I hate buses. They pull in at every stop. They never charge through amber lights, even though they have ample power and size. People board slowly. Then the bus waits for a green light. Or the driver sees someone running from a block away. Then the light turns red again. Public transit is for losers. Without my iPod, it's like being entombed alive.

My father is an ignorant turtle. He may be a soldier who can fight, but he never goes downtown. To him, it's full of poor people and drug addicts who carry guns and knives to rob you. Maybe that's why he kicked me out. He wants me to go there and get murdered. He wants a son who will become a doctor. Too bad my grades are low. Now he has an excuse to get rid of me.

I won't lie down and die. I'll survive and make him sorry for this. I'll show him that I'm better than him. Me, I know more than he does about this city. He can't even ride the subway! Me, I've gone downtown many times. The last time was to get a cool gift for Kevin's birthday.

———

I get off at Wellesley Station. This summer, our Chinese TV reporters came here for the Gay Pride festival. A long escalator lifts me slowly to the street. I don't know this part of the city and don't know where to go. But Ba kicked me out for being gay, so here I am.

I don't care what you think, you old fart. I don't care if you hate me.

First I check the map. Church Street was the site of marching bands, rainbow balloons and half-naked men dancing on floats. We laughed when one nervous reporter dropped his mike while talking to men dressed as glamorous women. Jenny wanted to go down and see, but Mila didn't.

In front of the station, vendors sell hotdogs, flowers and homemade jewelry. The tall buildings, busy stores and masses of people are like my hometown Beijing.

My feet are suddenly rubbery and heavy. I've never come downtown alone. I should have grabbed my pen-knife from my desk for protection. I reach inside my jacket and touch my wallet. My bankcard and cash will keep me safe, let me do whatever I want. I don't need to be afraid.

Students shuffle past in ragged groups, office workers rush by with shiny leather bags, and seniors riding motor chairs scoot through the crowds. Everyone talks on a cell.

I know Yonge Street, which lies in the other direction. Jian's girlfriend, Carla, marched there once in a happy parade of Christian church people. He and I walked beside her, waving little flags telling everyone that "Jesus Loves You." The street's little shops sell kinky is-this-legal stuff. Goth clerks pierce their faces full of metal.

The Yonge Street coffee bar is full of students and workers, but they're cool and hip in the latest shoes and jeans. At least one laptop sits on each table. Best of all, the music is a bit edgy.

It feels safe here. But when I buy coffee and a sandwich, my appetite vanishes.

I never eat sandwiches. None of my friends eat sandwiches.

Outside, cars crawl by. A man on a unicycle jerks and zigzags along, legs pumping forward then back, forward then back. Ba would sneer at him. But I like it downtown. Here, customers tap into the coffee bar's electricity for their laptops. It's considered good for business. At the Milky Way, the owner covered the electrical outlets with tape.

I log onto *Rebel State*. Monkey and Long Range complain they couldn't reach me earlier. The beach battle was delayed because not enough teams showed up. Central unveils its new weapons: Reflect Armor for its soldiers and Attack Wolves. Steel pauses to figure out how to handle them. Between skirmishes, I find the rest of my team: Heaven Hand and Trader. Normally I try not to kill enemy soldiers. Instead I injure them so they cannot wage war again. I earn Honor, not Blood.

The sudden blare of a car horn jolts me. Night has fallen. I lean back and rub my stiff neck. My scores for both Blood and Honor have both risen. I log off.

I love rolling in the thick blanket of *Rebel State*. Time sails by! You need skill and brains to survive. Steel's problems are real ones. How do you gain Honor while staying true to The Code? Do you keep playing when you lose Blood?

I eat my rock-hard sandwich. On the sound system, a saxophone plays a light, tricky tune.

At home about this time, I'd be in a panic about homework, having spent my time gaming and surfing for music. I'd be waiting for Niang to bring leftovers from the restaurant. She'll switch on the Chinese TV station and ask Ba to massage her feet. That's when I leave the room.

Store windows across the street reflect neon signs. On the road, lines of cars glow red and yellow. Around me, people continue to stare at laptops and sway to their earphones. A café worker clatters by with a tray of dirty dishes.

Up north, it's closing time, too. Head Cook prepares the end-of-day staff meal as Niang clears the cash register. All day she chats with customers young and old, even my friends. She knows people's names, birthdays, dates of first arrival in Canada, and most recent visits to China. People bring her gifts from China. She looks good, even without makeup. She can easily hook a rich man. So why does she stay with Ba?

For sex?

Ugh!

She's the best thing that ever happened to Ba. Graciously, she calls him her business partner when really he is waiter, kitchen help and delivery man. He is happiest when the phone rings with take-out orders and he can go play with his GPS. If Uncle Bei calls for food, then Ba is gone for several hours. That, believe it or not, is good for business. Niang can talk more freely with the male customers.

Jian gets tables with westerners because his English is best among the waiters. Customers give him better tips because he smiles more.

I hate grinning at strangers and hoping that they'll come back to eat again. Niang likes rich Chinese who order the pricey dishes. She chats them up, flatters them and makes them laugh. They treat me like dirt when I pour water and remove their plates. To them, waiters and busboys are immigrants who have failed. Luckily, Jian and I are called in only once a week now, so that we get time to study.

The coffee bar worker passes by again. This round, he stops and says, "...blah-blah-something-something-nine."

Slow down!

My ESL teacher said, "Just say 'Pardon me?' and people will repeat themselves. Don't worry, they don't mind."

Huh! The last time I did that, the server at the food court rolled her eyes to the ceiling and then leaned sideways to peer at the line-up behind me.

My laptop is fully charged now, and I scroll through my machine. What I really want is to visit the *Rebel State* forum but there's no time. The game is in Chinese. When I chat and argue there, that's the only time I feel I know anything for sure.

When you speak your own language, you can laugh and debate. At school, if you can't speak, you melt into the wall like paint.

Teachers point at us immigrants and say, "Speak up, the class wants to hear you. We really do!"

One day in English, the class read a play together. Each student had to read aloud as we went through the lines. Everyone was bored. No one paid attention until I reached the word "awry." I must have said it wrong because the entire class burst out laughing as if it was the funniest thing they had ever heard. I thought they were too bored to care. Even the teacher smiled.

People wait to jump on our mistakes.

I open a new page to make a plan.

1. Hide computer.
2. Find sleeping spot.
3. Brush teeth with Ultrasonic toothbrush. Hah!

I log onto my bank account. There's $368.14, enough

for several months of *Rebel State*. It's all gift money that I've been saving.

I wash my coffee down with cold water. No customers are left. The coffee bar offers five kinds of sugar for people who stay all day and spend money. Big fat easy chairs rest under cones of soft light from living-room lamps.

I glance around, reach between my table and the sofa and slip my laptop into the stand bursting with magazines and newspapers.

Outside at the bus stop, three kids sit on the sidewalk in front of a fancy chocolate store. One calls out, "Spare some change?"

I drop cash into their paper cup and hear, "Thanks, man."

They seem surprised. I doubt that many Chinese people give them money. They're so young they could be from my school. The boys have thin beards. The girl wears a shiny stud in her nose. Their jeans are open at the knees for that ragged look that was hot when I first arrived in Canada four years ago. They appear well fed. No doubt their parents' credit cards are tucked into their back pockets.

On their blackened feet, the two boys wear cheap flip-flops. I would never sink so low. Those are for bath houses and swimming pools, and for peasants working illegally in the cities.

In China, Ma always gave money to beggars: children, men, women, young and old alike.

"Stop it!" Ba grumbled. "They're an organized ring! Those beggars are richer than you and me."

"It makes me feel good," Ma said. She clung to a simple thought. If you did good deeds, then good things happened to you.

Ba labeled her a fool. My friends take Ba's side. Downtown, when they see me stopping at vagrants, they grab me by the collar and pull me away. It's a joke to them. They have to save me from myself.

Two police officers stroll by in armored vests. Their billy clubs and leather holsters glow from streetlamps.

I step onto the road and peer into the distance, as if I am waiting for the streetcar. That will explain why a clean-cut kid like me is out here so late.

The lights in the coffee bar flicker and go off. Mr. Blah-blah-something-something-nine hurries out, turns the key and yanks the door to test the lock.

Thank you, sir. Keep my machine safe, all right?

He's not carrying anything, and he had no time to tidy the place. I know the routine. At our restaurant, the workers who leave right at closing time escape having to mop and disinfect the washrooms. Niang gets someone else to do it the next morning.

My cell has a stack of texts. Mila is giddy about a

new MV from Faye Wong. Wei forwards a link to a sexy upload from Korea. Kai rates it Hot-hot-hot-hot. Earlier, Jenny invited people to go for sushi. Carla tells people (again) about her Bible study group's next meeting. Kevin's family ate at a new restaurant on Highway 7, but he says the food sucked. Clinton heard about a house party over the weekend where someone pulled a knife. No one got hurt. Now he's asking to copy someone's biology homework.

Jian wants to know where I am. Probably Niang told him to ask.

I doubt that Ba told them the truth about kicking me out. Instead he'll say something stupid like, "That idiot son of mine yelled and cursed me, so I told him to get out. I didn't think he would, but he did. He was glad to leave."

Jian and Niang will know that Ba is lying, but they won't challenge him. They'll let him save face. Niang will get nervous about me but Ba will tell her, "Don't worry. I took care of myself when I was his age."

How do I explain this? There's no good gossip to share. I haven't had gay sex. I don't have a boyfriend. I didn't get drunk and pass out at a gay bar. I'm not like Tyson Somers, the vice-president of the student council who started the year by telling the whole world he's gay. He's handsome and on the football team. His father runs a Winners store and his mother is a lawyer. They stand behind him one hundred percent.

But hooligans kicked in Tyson's locker and emptied a can of paint over his stuff. Then, after a late afternoon football game, he got beat up so badly that he spent a night in hospital. He never named his attackers. Everyone at school thinks they were his former teammates on the football team.

That's the real world. Life is unfair. Some kids get everything while others have nothing. All my friends struggle with English but I'm the slowest. Mila's parents are divorced, too, but she's happy living with cousins and grandparents. Half my friends are virgins (even though they say they're not), but none of them are gay. Wei's parents run a restaurant, too, but they don't demand slave labor from him.

I shut my cell and breathe in the cool air. Freedom! I stroll with my back straight and arms loose but by my side. It is Steel's warrior walk. No hoodlum will hassle me.

The office towers are bright, their lights perched high up in airplane zone. Condo windows are fogged by the blurry colors of TV screens. Homeless people bed down in bus shelters and squat in bank-machine rooms, guarding their shopping carts. Those tiny spaces must stink. At 24-hour coffee shops, teens with rumpled hair and layers of clothes hang around tables. I won't go in there and have those kids snicker at me. How do such places make money?

I turn the corner and stop in my tracks. I stand still for only a half a second because I'm not a country bumpkin.

Western movies and TV all show hookers selling sex on streets just like this. I never thought I'd get so close. Real chickens strutting around! And on my first night on my own!

I watch from a bus stop. The women's short skirts and tight tops reveal bare skin and fleshy curves. They totter back and forth inside little borders of pavement. Even on high heels, they look mean enough to cause serious pain with a quick kick. Their noses leak cigarette smoke across painted faces. Cars slow down while dark windows protect the men inside.

The women give me a passing glance and stay away.

Last year, You-peng told me in an excited email that Beijing police arrested my former classmate Fan Min at a massage parlor. No wonder she could afford the high-end messaging service!

"She's a public bus," You-peng wrote. "Everyone gets on." He said the boys at school started to follow her around. She laughed and told them, "Come back when you can pay my prices."

I walk away. Maybe I should go to Church Street to watch young men do the same business. In China, boys who sell sex to men are called money boys, while those who offer services to women are called ducks.

I saw one such woman interviewed on China's national news. Her face was hidden. Sex with her husband was boring, she chirped, so she invited ducks to her home when her husband was at work. She declared that she wasn't cheating on him.

"Sex and love are separate things," she said. "I bring home ducks. We go to bed. No emotions are involved. But with my husband, there are feelings. I love him and he loves me. We have known each other all our lives!"

I shudder. If I don't go home, then money boy work may be *my* future.

———

In the alley behind the coffee bar, high lamps spread a spooky orange glow over the smells of restaurant garbage. Traffic sounds creep between the buildings. One loading bay has a deep platform with protective shadows.

I climb up and drop my backpack. Sitting down, I picture myself at the Milky Way Café with Kai and Wei, Mila and Jenny, sipping ice coffees. Mine is black, no cream and no sugar. A tough guy's drink.

"Ba tells me to get out, so I curse him and leave," I

will say. "I go downtown, hang around and then bed down behind the coffee shop. No trouble at all, as long as you don't mind peeing outside."

"Why didn't you call us?" they'll ask.

"I ran out of the house so fast I didn't grab my cell."

I take my cell and stare at it. Kai will let me stay at his place if I ask. His father is working in China now, and his mother enjoys having another male around the house. But she's a nervous busybody. She'll want to talk to Ba or Stepmother to make sure they know where I am.

If Ba doesn't know where I am, he'll worry about me. And then he'll be sorry for what he did.

The cold floor sucks away my body heat. Can I sneak into the garage at home and sleep there? I know the code. For sure it's warmer than this place. But if Ba finds me there, he'll have won. No way will that happen.

A strong light pokes into my eyes. I block it out with my hands. Cops?

"Sir, are you okay?" someone shouts.

Am I being arrested? I turn my head away. Will I end up in jail?

"I'm not a cop," a man calls out, coming closer. "I'm with Street Outreach."

I smell coffee.

"Sir, you want something hot to drink?" he asks.

I pull my baseball cap down over my face. The man

mustn't see that I'm a kid. I push back my shoulders to look bigger.

"Sir, this isn't a safe place."

I can take care of myself!

Finally he says, "Okay, I'm going. Here's my card, all right? If you change your mind and need a place to stay, come look us up. We're not far away. Have a good night, eh?"

I can't go with him. Immigrants take care of themselves. If we come and use the welfare system, then other Chinese will have a harder time getting into Canada. That's what Niang says.

You can't get angry at Canadians for being helpful. They truly care about the old and the weak, the homeless, the refugees. They help all needy people. High-paid lawyers speak out for them! I'll gladly pay taxes, if Stepmother would only pay me regular wages. I hate asking Ba for money, but I do.

I'll be Steel and make my way through these downtown canyons the same way he slides along steep cliffs using only ropes and muscle.

When teachers get frustrated, they shake their heads and say, "You young people, take a walk in the real world. See how tough life really is!"

Now I am.

———

I awake to pitch black. Pain jabs me, but where, exactly? My head? My knee?

My senses spring alert. I hear heavy breathing. The back of my neck chafes at cold concrete.

Ow! My head bangs the wall. My arms are paralyzed. What happened to them? My lips move but no sound comes out.

A sharp tip pricks my throat. Something smooth and cold slides across my chin. I flinch.

"Money!" hisses a voice. "Where's your money?"

I shake my head and try to shout, "No money," but someone with a monstrous hand grips my head like a bowling ball. Then he grabs my throat. I inhale cigarettes and liquor and shit. I thrash about, but my attacker is big and solid as a bear.

"Money!" hisses the voice.

I tear madly at my clothes. My wallet is next to my skin, at my belt. I fumble it like a hot potato. A second later, the attacker and my wallet are gone.

My entire body is shaking. I can't stop it. I rub my hands together. Finally I force myself to get up and walk back and forth.

Stop shaking, I shout at myself. Some warrior.

All the self-defense that Ba taught me long ago comes flooding into my head. I should have twisted and rolled. I should have kicked out.

Ba should have drilled me harder.
The shrill wail of sirens rises in the distance.
Fire engine? Ambulance?
I hope they're coming for me.
I don't want to be out here anymore.

Four

I stay awake all night. I need to be ready to fight off a second attacker. In truth, the moment I let my eyelids drop, I feel a cold blade at my neck and my eyes fly open.

I jump up and think to go find a safer, brighter place. How about that 24-hour coffee shop?

Why bother?

The danger is gone. Why defend a fortress after the enemy has driven your soldiers into the forest?

I grope around for my cell. I can't find it.

Was I stupid or what? Sleeping outside. I want to punch and kick myself. But my body already aches all over.

A year ago I was at the cash register when someone came into the restaurant. His brown leather jacket was low-grade material, stiff and cracking. The red baseball cap had seen too much sun. He didn't belong in our neighborhood. He had that nervous smile of westerners who don't know if we Chinese speak any English.

Instead he propped one elbow on the counter to cradle a gleaming gun and pointed it straight at me. He slid a paper bag over the glass.

"Give...me...the...money." His words rolled out slowly.

I was so surprised to have understood him that I froze. But he didn't praise my English skills. He leaned forward, shoved the gun into my gut and muttered, "Money! Now!"

He smelled of cheap hair gel. I yanked out bills and filled his bag. He started to back away, still pointing his gun at me. I put my hands up even though he hadn't said to do that.

Ba silently slid in behind him. He was barefoot. In one move he seized the robber's wrist, twisted and yanked it high behind him. The gun clattered to the floor. Ba kicked it away and grabbed the paper bag. The robber broke away and sprinted out the door. Ba dashed after him but limped back a second later. Niang came running with his shoes and socks.

"Someone was waiting in a car," he reported. "Rotting hooligans!"

The police warned Ba never to do this again. Stopping an armed robbery and chasing the robbers was far too dangerous.

"What if he had opened fire?" they said over and over. "The boy might have gotten shot. Or your customers."

Ba explained that he was an army man and a former police officer who knew exactly what he was doing. The cops didn't try to understand Ba's English. They didn't respect China's army or police. Ba cursed them as they left, calling them sissies.

I remember thinking that being shot and killed would be the perfect escape for me. I hated living here. People would think of me forever as an innocent young man, cut down at the prime of life. All that fine education wasted. All those advantages lost. Ba would regret forcing me to move to Canada. He'd admit he was wrong to bully me about studying. He'd wish he hadn't put such strict rules on my life, and finally confess, "My son and I, we both could have been happier, had I only been a better father."

Then he would break down sobbing.

Ma would travel from China for my funeral. She would shriek with grief, throw herself onto my coffin and refuse to let go. Grandfather would wail about the family line coming to an end.

One by one my friends would drop long-stemmed roses into my grave while my hard-hearted teachers hid their tears at failing to understand me. Maybe some westerner kids would show up. My school would honor me with a minute of silence.

In reality, I sat on the toilet in the restaurant men's room, arms wrapped tight around my sides. Tears streamed down my face. I couldn't let anyone see. I couldn't blow my nose in case someone heard me.

Why was I blubbering like a baby? No one blamed me. The police said I had done the right thing. No one was hurt. Our money was safe. Ba's quick thinking had saved us all.

Wasn't that how the universe was supposed to unfold?

I don't move until the rectangle of sky over the alley brightens from black to gray and then to white. A delivery van roars by, skids and sprays gravel against my wall. Crazy driver. My stomach is knotted and my back aches.

A flash of red catches my eye. My backpack sits in an oily, greenish puddle. My clothes are scattered across the alley.

First they were strewn across our lawn, and now this. Heaven intended them to get lots of fresh air.

I run and gather my wet, gritty clothes. My watch isn't on my wrist. I check the loading bay. Nothing.

My cellphone is gone, too.

How will my family track me down if I don't have a cell? How will Ba beg me to come home?

For half a second I smile grimly. What if Ba phones

me and winds up talking to the mugger? They can't understand each other. They scream back and forth, swearing in two languages.

They deserve each other. They can drive each other crazy.

I dust off my jacket, but last night's scuffle sanded down the sheen of the nylon. Now I look grubby.

Around the corner, a rush of warm traffic air hits my face. The coffee bar is open. Pot-lamps brighten the window despite plenty of natural light. Office workers block the counter. I hold the door open for a woman wearing a pencil-thin suit and fruity perfume. She doesn't bother to thank me.

The space between my table and the big fat easy chair is empty. The magazine stand is gone! I spin around. My backpack crashes into people. They frown and fall back as if I'm diseased.

The stand is in the corner, by the other window. I rush across the room. More newspapers have been stuffed in. They stick out in a lopsided fan.

I dig in. I pull out my laptop and clutch it to my chest. The saxophone music from yesterday suddenly comes on.

Maybe heaven is watching out for me after all, like that three-eyed god at the temple we invaded in *Rebel State*.

In the washroom, I thrust my hands under the hot water and swallow several mouthfuls, hoping the warmth will soothe my stomach. In the mirror, my face is pale and dirty. No new pimples, lucky me. My short hair sticks up like a brush while dark rings hang beneath my eyes. My lips need cream.

In my pocket, I find 63 cents and three student bus tickets.

There's just enough money for one phone call.

———

First I visit my bank in the little plaza across from the one holding our restaurant. I rarely come to the branch, even though its workers are all Chinese. I prefer bank machines. I hate line-ups. Many customers are seniors with hearing and loneliness problems, and they need hours of hand-holding from the tellers.

"You look like a goddess." I speak Chinese to a teller with long straight hair. "I hope you can save my life."

"Of course I'll help you," she giggles. She's very young, and flat as an airplane runway.

I explain my situation and try to catch her eye, to see if she will flirt. It's easy to play the game with girls from China. The rules are simple. Guys talk tough and girls act tiny.

She hurries away on loud heels, and then an older

woman, a four-eyed frog, is demanding my ID.

"I told her I lost my wallet," I say. "How can I give you any ID?"

She taps quickly on the computer.

"Who is Chen Hai-hua?" she asks.

"My mother. My stepmother."

"Why didn't you bring her along?" She wears a jade pendant far too green to be real.

"Why? This is my account."

"She must sign an authorization. Or I cannot help you."

"Let me tell you my code number," I offer.

"You must show me the card."

"Don't other people lose wallets? What do you do then?"

"Check their signature."

Oh. I never signed anything here. Stepmother opened the account for me. I refused to come here with her. That was when we first arrived four years ago and I wanted to go back to China.

"It's not so difficult, is it?" The woman smiles at me. "Your mother doesn't work far away. Just bring her over."

I curse her noble ancestors to the eighth generation. Under my breath, of course.

———

The food court at North Star Mall is crowded with after-school kids. I don't want to be here. It's too close to school. The last thing I want is to bump into someone I know. But Jian insisted on meeting here.

Luckily the food court is strictly western food, so chances are small that my friends might show. Just to be safe, I stand behind a pillar.

The mall's fountain shoots out jets of colored water timed to military music. Mothers tell their toddlers to watch the dancing foam.

The smell of fresh baking and hot tomato sauce makes my mouth water. I've loved pizza all my life, even in China.

I spot a Chinese grandfather and grandson at a nearby table. The boy looks nine or ten. The old man raises a slice of pizza to the boy's mouth. The boy clamps his mouth shut and shakes his head. The grandfather sighs. With a plastic fork, he spears two French fries, coats them with ketchup and holds them to the boy's mouth. Again he refuses the food.

The old man angrily pitches away the fork. He offers the boy a drink from the straw. No again. Then he zips the boy into a puffy bomber jacket. He stands up and drags the boy away. They leave behind plenty of food.

My feet start walking with a mind of their own. They'll take me to that table. I'll sit and pretend to be saving the table for friends. I'll wave to them as they wait at a counter for food. Then, absently, I'll pick at the food and slip pieces into my mouth.

There's sharp applause behind me as the water show ends. I hurry back to the pillar.

I can't be seen eating other people's slop. I can't give westerners another reason to laugh at Chinese people.

That grandfather and grandson remind me of millions of parents in China trying to buy their children's obedience with western food. Ma did the same, but she loved that food, too.

Grandfather never used food or money to bribe me. When I was about eight or nine, I told him that all my friends had grandparents who bought them western fast food as treats. He said, "I'm your grandfather, not your friends' grandfather."

And he told Ba to follow his example, not Ma's.

Growing up, I heard Ma tell her fast-food story so often that it's now carved into my brain. Her sixteenth birthday landed on the same day that KFC opened its first outlet in China. She insisted that friends take her to Qianmen Street. She had to see the biggest KFC restaurant in the world. The line-up stretched to Tiananmen Square. Their bill came to 192 yuan.

Her face lit up when she recalled all this. That was the best day of her life.

My hands are sticky with sweat. A part of me worries that Jian may not come. We aren't close like the good-hearted brothers we see on western TV. We don't do homework together even though that would save time for both of us. Jian thinks only losers get hooked on on-line role-play games. Ba always crows about how perfect Jian is.

"If you spoke English half as well as him," Ba says to me, "then you would have no problems."

"Look at Jian's report card! He will get many scholarships for college."

"How many sports trophies did Jian win? Look at you, you're useless!"

Is it my fault that our school has no gymnastics team?

Too bad Ba doesn't know that Jian hates him as much as I do. Ba the army man orders everyone around. "No discipline, no civilization" is one of his stupid mottos.

Jian wants to sleep in and to stay out late, too. He has a girlfriend, Carla, which is the big secret we keep from our parents. Ba and Niang insist that girls and sex come later, after college, when they cannot distract you from winning a big-money future.

I see Jian coming from afar. He is tall enough for the school basketball team, and his spiky hair makes him taller. He has a boxy, rugged face and looks like an actor. Girls chased him even in China.

Things are so easy for him. Niang adores him and talks to him like an adult, a friend. He can stumble through life with a blindfold and still reach the top of the heap. He is everything I want to be. Handsome. Straight. Ex-virgin.

I wave at Jian. Then I see Carla beside him.

Rot! How are we going to have a private chat?

Carla dashes up and gives me a hug. It warms me right down to my toes. Now I'm glad she came. I stand still. She smells delicious. There's lemon and spices in her shampoo.

Before Jian can speak, I drag him to the nearest food counter.

"You brought money?" I ask.

He nods as I complain about yesterday's sandwich. We both hate western-style bread. That's all we have in common.

"You look awful," he says, frowning. "Didn't you sleep?"

We take away two trays heaped with fried chicken, fries and salad. I tear into the food like an animal.

"Your father said you were cocky." Jian speaks as soon as we sit. "He said he told you to quit your computer game but you wouldn't, so he kicked you out. Is that what happened?"

I nod. The last thing I want is for the gang to know about me.

One day Tyson and his friends walked by us in the hallway. Mila raised two fingers to the back of her head and pointed them up. Then she wiggled her nose and made a joke about spitting on rabbits. Everyone laughed, even me. In China, gay men are called rabbits. People there don't want homosexuals in their families.

"Your ba didn't work last night. Old Lin filled in. Ma called me today and said he stayed in bed all morning. Old Lin will cover for him again. Ma's not happy at all."

"Lazy turtle egg," I mutter. We speak quietly, as teens do when using Chinese in public. Our adults are the ones who speak far too loud.

"Where were you last night?" Jian asks.

I shake my head. My mouth is full.

"Can't you apologize to your ba?" Jian asks. "Every time he gets in a bad mood, my ma gets stressed out. I don't care that she snaps at me, but it's hard on the workers at the restaurant, too."

Not my problem. Niang worries too much about everything. I'm sure Ba told her about me. But I'm his son, not hers, so he'll have to deal with me.

I keep eating. Finally I say, "Can you lend me some money?"

"You should go home! Your father loves you!" Carla's Mandarin is clumsy. Her parents are from Hong Kong, so she speaks Cantonese and English. Her Mandarin came from watching Chinese movies and TV series. She and Jian are in an after-school program, studying how to write exams to get into U.S. colleges. Ba brags about this to his friends.

When I ignore her, Jian says, "What about school? You can't skip more classes. Your ba will chop off your head."

"Just lend me some money." I'm begging, but now I have an excuse to quit school. I have to start working in order to provide for myself.

He digs out some ten- and twenty-dollar bills.

"I'll pay you back," I say. "I promise."

"Go say sorry to your father," Jian says. "You can't last long away from home."

Carla hands me two twenty-dollar bills. I'm surprised.

"I'll pray for you," she says. "Don't worry. Our Heavenly Father will look after you."

She lowers her head to pray, right there.

If I had a girlfriend, she should be exactly like Carla. Her long black hair shines as if her head contains batteries to power the glow. She speaks perfect English to her westerner friends, and jokes with the westerner teachers. Kids like her usually don't care if you are gay or straight or have a green polka-dot face.

But Carla and her family are serious church-goers. At a school rally held to support Tyson after he got out of hospital, Carla and her friends held up signs that quoted the Bible. They called gay people sinners. Some students booed them. But Mila and the gang kept quiet.

I don't want to cause trouble between Jian and Carla. She's on the honor roll and helps him study and climb up the education mountain. No way can I tell them about me.

"What next?" Jian sounds impatient. His gaze wanders around the food court. "You can't stay on your own forever."

"I'll go back to China," I declare.

"No, you won't! What about airfare?"

"My ma will pay."

Jian frowns and gets up to stretch. The plastic chairs are hard.

"You're a stubborn donkey," he says. "Just come home."

"No."

"You're stupid if you go back to China. You have a better future here."

"You sound like Ba."

After they leave, I pour every last crumb of chicken into my mouth. I empty all the packets of ketchup and soak my fries in them. I even scrape clean the salad containers.

I half thought Ba would send a message with Jian, saying sorry and telling me to come home. But he's hiding in bed and making people worry about him. As if he's the victim!

I'm going home to China. I'll move in with Ma for a while and meet up with my old friends. I'll get a job and start saving up for my own place. Everyone says China's economy is booming.

I use Jian's money to buy a telephone card. At a public telephone, I press Ma's number. The ringing goes on and on. There's no answer at her end, not even an answering machine.

Truth is, Ma may not be able to help.

In between her department store jobs, Ma learned to play on-line poker from her friends. She loved it. Ba lived at the army base and traveled for work, so she gambled all day and all night. One time she played for such high stakes that she forgot to pick me up from school. The teacher left me standing outside the building and told the doorman to keep an eye on me.

One day Grandfather took me to Second Aunt's place, Ba's sister. She had a bigger apartment, fancy furniture and a better TV than us. I fell asleep there. Then I overheard Second Aunt tell someone on the telephone that Ma owed money from gambling and was selling tofu to pay it off. When I asked Ma, she laughed and said I had misheard. Soon she quit playing poker.

When I was eleven, in middle school, Ba and Ma

divorced. If Ma had been a better wife, then Ba would never have gotten interested in Niang. Ma hated waking up early and got fired from her department store jobs. She wanted to stay home and watch TV. When Ba came home from his tours of duty, he would mop the floors and wash the windows. He said he liked how everything in the army was neat and tidy.

Ma knew I wanted to live with her yet she didn't fight to keep me. Instead she handed me to Ba like a store clerk passing out leaflets on the street. It took Grandfather twice as long to ride the buses to Niang's home to visit me, so he didn't see me as much as before.

"Sons always follow fathers," Ma insisted. "You carry his surname."

"What about Jian?" I retorted. "He follows his mother."

"Oh, his father has children with several women. He cares nothing about Jian. But don't ever say that to him."

At school, I heard that selling tofu referred to women who sold their bodies for sex. But I didn't want to think that Ma had done it. I wanted to go live with her, especially after Ba and Niang announced plans to go to Canada.

I didn't see Ma again until the airport. She hugged me and soaked her handkerchief with tears. I thought, if she's so sad to see me go, then she should let me stay!

"I want to stay with you," I declared.

"Your father can give you a good life in Canada," she replied. "It is the best country in the world. Many people in China are emigrating."

"Ma, I don't want to go."

She shook her head and said, "Don't be silly. This is a wonderful opportunity."

When our flight was called, I held onto my plastic chair, which was bolted to the floor. Ma and her mother Popo begged me to let go. When Ba slapped my head, I yelped like a wounded animal. Travelers and children younger than me turned at the sudden sound. A little girl dropped her soft drink and began to wail.

"You shame our family," Ba hissed.

He fetched a security guard armed with a gleaming automatic rifle, a pistol in a holster, headset, microphone and face shield. The soldier knelt and said if I did not go with Ba, I would be sent to a reform school for young criminals.

That's how my journey to Canada started.

Five

The afternoon is late when I reach the homeless shelter. I found it on the net. One blog said this is the biggest and the best, even though it is run by a church.

At first I'm excited at finding the place. Now I want to vanish. I don't enjoy walking into serious places by myself. This is a first for me. Immigrants are toddlers who get led everywhere by the hand. An immigrant consultant helped Jian and me register for school. Our neighbor Mrs. Lo showed us the library and community center.

It's just a building, I tell myself. There are Canadians and social workers inside, not Chinese door guards or police officers. Immigrants can't be cowards, isn't that so? And I'm not sleeping outside again!

Last night I was too proud for charity. Not anymore. The building has three stories that stretch down the block and around the corner. So many people have gone in that I don't think I'll be noticed.

Inside, strong lamps light up the hallway. It glows with warmth. The waxed floor is shiny and the big door-mat looks new. A wide hallway lets people move in and out quickly. Someone bumps into me. I step aside.

On the walls are big posters promoting the four food groups, safe sex, multiculturalism, and the need to quit smoking. A bulletin board is crowded with messages asking for help.

Have you seen this man? He's missing.

My baby will be born soon. I need a bigger apartment.

I'm looking for office work that doesn't involve computers.

I peer into a sweet-smelling dining room. People are lining up for food. The sign says if you want to stay overnight, then you must register. That involves a line-up, too.

The place reminds me of my community center up north, where we sometimes play basketball during free gym times. It's always noisy there, with kids chasing and screaming. Ba would enjoy this place and its peace and order.

Where do I hide my laptop? We're in a shabby district away from the downtown businesses. The stores and res-taurants look low-class and dingy, so of course criminals and thieves are around.

The office door opens and someone leaves. A moment later, a voice calls for the next person in line.

Inside, I see a woman's arched back in a long dress. She is bent over, peering into a filing cabinet.

"Have a seat." Her voice is rich, strong and accented.

She turns around. She is the most beautiful African woman I have ever seen. Her eyes are enormous and her cheekbones are high. Her hair is tightly braided in tiny coils over her head, and her face is heart-shaped.

How is it that such a woman works here? She should be in the movies!

She frowns at my staring and pushes plastic sheet protectors toward me.

"Are you hungry?" She speaks slowly, holding up a picture of a busy cafeteria.

"No need for this." I wave away the photo. "I know English."

"We serve hot meals, for free," she says. "Anyone, doesn't matter who you are, can come in and eat."

Her sentences are slow so I understand every word.

"You need clothes?"

"You need a doctor?"

"Are you on drugs?"

"Have you stayed at a shelter before?"

"Need to wash your clothes? We have washers and dryers you can use, for free."

Finally I say yes. She smiles happily.

She asks me for ID.

Uh-oh.

"I lost them." I expect to be marched to the exit.

She shrugs. "We'll help you get some tomorrow."

After filling in a one-page form, I'm taken upstairs. The clerk hands me a towel, shaving gear and locker key. My room holds eight sets of bunkbeds. Two men are present.

One man is bent over, clipping his toenails. At every loud click, sharp blackened pieces shoot across the room. The man's foot is pink and yellowish, and also dark and bruised in spots. I glance away and look for a faraway bed.

The other man looks as if he just survived a storm in a forest. His rain parka, jeans and boots are streaked with mud and other stains. Under his hood, a grubby red toque is pulled down to the neck. His arms are wrapped around his body, as if he's cold. He's bent over, too, facing the floor with closed eyes. I walk around him.

"Don't worry," the clerk tells me with a wave of his hand. "This one is praying, and the other man is harmless. They've both stayed here before."

I jump to a top bunk. It'll be harder for thieves to get up here. There are no ladders. The mattress feels good, more hard than soft. On the walls, people used pens and markers to write their names and dates of stay here. I don't see any Chinese names.

I'm a homeless person now. In China, city folk complain about homeless people and tell them to go back to their villages. There are too many of them clogging the train and bus stations and sleeping under freeway overpasses and in McDonald's restaurants. They're accused of stealing and robbing, of taking advantage of city people.

I don't know what to expect at this shelter. So far, so good.

After a quick shower, I put on my cleanest clothes and hurry to the dining room. Teenagers stand behind the stainless-steel counter, their long hair crammed under net hats, to help dish out the food. They must be earning community service credits. There's soup, brown bread, beef stew, carrots, beans and a fruit salad.

I stare down at my tray of food. Truth is, I don't want those teenagers to see me. What will they think?

There are no empty tables, so I drop into the nearest seat. I shove food into my mouth and keep my head down. A priest and nun stroll through and chat with diners.

A man at the far table catches my eye. It's his white shirt, business tie and dark jacket that I notice. He has wide shoulders and black-framed eyeglasses. He dabs his mouth with a napkin each time he stops eating.

What is this well-groomed man doing here? He should be presenting the news on TV.

When I go for seconds, I walk toward him. Then I see that the collar of his white shirt is frayed and yellowing. His tie is crumpled. His jacket doesn't match the pants. One hand trembles as he raises his cup. The drink almost spills. The nearby men talk to one another but not him.

The men at my table have decided to dislike me. They pretend to talk to each other but they speak so loudly that it's clear they want me to hear them. They blame the government, young people and the economy for all their problems. One man hurt his back while working, but no lawyer will help him sue his boss. A second man has looked for a job for over two years. The third man wishes he was young again.

Then I hear the words "damn immigrants."

The first English word I learned in Canada was immigrant. It warned me that people nearby were talking about me. Soon I learned more words that signaled danger: newcomer, foreigner, alien, refugee. It was a long list, as if Canadians had many complaints about us.

But we create jobs. If not, Canada wouldn't take immigrants. Niang has eleven employees. They all pay taxes.

These men should shut up. But can I say anything?

Abruptly they stop talking. The priest tells us that

the drop-in center is showing a movie tonight. He says welcome to me and asks how I'm doing.

Westerners, especially ones who push me to talk, make me nervous. I keep my mouth shut.

I take my clothes downstairs and head toward the sharp smell of bleach. Between the washers and dryers are two worn sofas filled with older men. They nod at me. Two of them play a card game, shouting with glee each time they smack down a card. The others flip through tattered magazines. The smell of cigarettes is strong, even though a No Smoking sign hangs over them.

A man waves at me. "Hey, kid, want to sit down?"

"No, thank you."

"Don't be shy. Take a load off your feet."

No.

"Come say hello to your cousin here," he says.

They all laugh.

The First Nations person next to Joker punches him.

"Shut up," he growls. "That kid, he's not my cousin. He's your uncle!"

Joker lurches from the room.

I take a deep breath. Was that a joke or insult?

If I get angry, then I'm young and lack self-control. I need to be an adult and show no weakness. At school, silence is seen as stupidity, because silence means you can't speak English properly. But here, silence is power.

It means you don't care what other people are thinking or saying.

My clothes swim round and round in the machine. If only life was this simple. Throw in dirty clothes, pour in detergent and push a button. The water fills up, hot as you want. Set the dial at Heavy Duty to scrub out bad stains. Half an hour later, all is clean and fresh. You're a new person.

One man is folding clothes from the dryer. The loose tanktop he wears makes him look scrawny, but big bones stick out from his shoulders. His skin hangs loose but it must have held plenty of weight and muscle in the past. He looks up.

"Don't worry, son." His voice booms out. His words are slurred and slow. "Things will work out."

I glance around. Who's he talking to? I'm not his son!

"Life stinks now," he continues. "But stand back for a moment. Then take the high road. Don't do anything you might regret."

I roll my eyes to the ceiling. What's a loser like him telling me what to do?

On the main floor, men are gathered around a TV for the movie. It's something I saw years ago dubbed into Chinese. Julia Roberts' gay friend goes with her to a wedding.

The movie has reached the restaurant scene. The gay

friend starts singing. There's no music. Family members join in, as do waiters and diners at other tables. My friends and I, we laughed and cheered, too, as if we understood the plot, even when Julia Roberts didn't win back the man she loved. Everything from Hollywood made sense, right?

"This frigging movie is for girls!" a man cries out. "Get something for men!"

"This is the best picture I ever saw," someone shouts.

"Shut up, faggot."

"Suck my dick!"

"Shut up, both of you!" A third voice rings out.

There's a loud clatter of metal chairs hitting the floor as men leap to their feet. A shelter worker comes running.

Crazy! The men get free food and beds here but all they do is make trouble!

I hurry upstairs and get into bed. I keep my pants on, just in case there's a need to run.

I'm dead tired but sleep won't come. One man snores loudly. His bunkmate coughs until he sits up and clears his throat into a towel. Another man argues loudly with himself, swearing at people's names. Every hour, the man in the bunk below me shuffles to the bathroom. He reeks of alcohol, even though no liquor is allowed. Down the hall, a door creaks every time it opens.

Even with a pillow over my head, I'm wide awake. The sounds of men muttering and farting grow louder. My feet stay cold even inside my socks. I hear the streetcar rolling over steel rails outside.

There's no way I'll stay another night. Here, I'm small and cornered. In *Rebel State*, I can fight my way through danger and hardship to win Honor. But in real life, I reached Canada too late. I'll never win anything here.

I need to get out. Where do I go? I only have about a hundred dollars. It won't last long.

Next morning, the cafeteria serves oatmeal and toast, hard-boiled eggs and peanut butter, tea and coffee. I'm not hungry but I force myself to eat.

At the pay phone, I punch in the numbers for China again. I glance at the clock. In Beijing, it's dinner time. This time Ma answers.

When I hear her voice, my body stiffens. There's no telling what mood she's in. When I was small, nothing scared me more than her sudden flashes of anger. One minute she would be normal and quiet. The next minute she would be cursing and stomping around the room.

I swallow hard and grip the telephone tightly. The last time we talked was on my birthday earlier this year.

Then it was my turn to phone back, but I got busy and kept forgetting.

There's background noise at her end, so I have to shout my name.

"Ma, how are you?"

"Same. How are you doing at school?"

"Same." She doesn't sound happy to hear from me.

"You need to study harder. You'll feel better when you get good marks, isn't that so? Do you miss me?"

"Yes." I know that's the right thing to say.

"Will you come home for New Year?"

"That would be great! Of course I'll come." Relief and joy fill me. It's just a few months away.

"No," Ma says abruptly. "Not a good time. I promised Popo I would go home for New Year. I didn't see my mother at all this year."

"I can go with you," I insist. But it's a lost battle. Ma's invitation was never sincere.

"You hate the village."

"I want to see Popo," I wail like a five-year-old.

"When you finish the term, come for summer holidays. How many years of school do you have left?"

"Two," I say, deflated.

"How's your father?"

"He's fine. He's busy. Ma, I need money. I have extra expenses, at school."

"Yes, yes, of course, I'll send money," she says. "But I must go now. I'm busy at work."

Work? What kind of work? I want to ask but she's gone.

I lean my back to the wall and bang my fist into it. Why doesn't my own mother know what grade I'm in?

She's my mother. She brought me into this world. I didn't ask to be born. She has to help me out. That's her job. She lives halfway around the world but that doesn't cancel her responsibilities. She owes me big.

I sit by the office and wait for it to open so that someone can get me some ID. My laptop delivers messages from all my friends. Wei and Jenny want to know where I am and why I'm not answering their texts. They wonder what big secret Jian, Carla and I are hiding from them. They ask if my parents know that I'm skipping school. Joey Xie is organizing a surprise party for his girlfriend's birthday. Don't I think that Julie's haircut is hideous? And where do we want to meet for lunch today?

My fingers itch for my cell, to tap out messages, to catch up with pals.

Could you live if you were chopped off at the wrist? No, you bleed to death.

I log onto the game and get directed to the forum. Rebel Command is giving up the fortress. It plans to launch a guerrilla war to attack weaker parts of the enemy, sabotage its supply lines and break its morale.

That kind of a war is bad for the local people, I tap in confidently. The enemy punishes them after our attacks, enslaves them. The people can't protect themselves. They want a final battle that leads to peace. They don't want war to go on forever.

I will lead an army, I declare. *Warriors who want a battle, follow me!*

Someone challenges me. *Rebel Command is right*, he posts. *This way, more of our teams and soldiers will survive.*

Coward, I retort. *You're afraid to fight and die.*

No, Steel, you're the coward. You fear failure. You would rather die quickly than work slowly to reduce the enemy's power. Besides, what do you know about ordinary people? You were born into wealth.

My face reddens and my heart starts pounding loudly, even though this chat takes place through cyberspace with total strangers.

People are siding with Rebel Command. I don't see any of my team members jumping in to support me. The generals will discharge me for challenging their orders.

Fart, I'm going to lose a big chunk of my Honor. Why am I being called a coward? I spoke out for the ordinary people! I should have won Honor instead!

"Good morning!" calls out the social worker as she arrives. A line-up of people has formed behind me. I log off, drag my backpack into the office and remind her of my problem.

"Do you have any ID?" she asks. "Driver's license, passport, Permanent Resident Card, social insurance number, bus pass?"

"No."

"Did anyone in your family write down those numbers?"

I shrug. Niang has my passport and PR card. My SIN card is in my desk somewhere.

"Have you any relatives who will sign a declaration attesting to your identity?"

I don't really understand her so I shake my head.

"I just need my bank card," I say. "Can you talk to my bank? I know my PIN number."

She shakes her head and writes down an address for me. "This is the Chinese immigrant agency, in Chinatown. Go tell them your problem. Maybe they can help you."

Yesterday she made getting new ID sound so simple.

And I don't want to go to Chinatown. That place is for losers.

Six

I was eager to see Church Street and the gay district, but they're as boring as any other street. People line up at bank machines. They take time to choose flowers from buckets. A panhandler holds out her baseball cap in front of the wine store. Trucks double park at stores and restaurants. Cars behind them honk impatiently.

I see coffee bars, pizza places and restaurants. No Chinese food, but there's sushi. A big drugstore fills one corner. The gift shop carries sexy birthday cards. Next door is a movie rental shop, but isn't everything on the Internet? Above the street are signs in windows for AIDS groups and the gay newspaper.

Finally I find something. The dimly lit store has the same new-clothes smell and loud music as in suburban malls. But the mannequins wear a lot of black leather clothing and flimsy underwear. The racks of uniforms for cops, soldiers, superheroes and Japanese schoolgirls are serious. It's no cheap Halloween display. The sign with a line across its red circle declares *Customers must be age eighteen and over.* It makes me feel like I belong here. Under it are rows of rubber models of body parts. They look very real. The super-size ones are amazing.

Where's my cell? I should send pictures to Ba. Show him more of his new homeland.

A hardware store and a little park are farther up on Church, so it feels different from Yonge Street's trendy shops. The Gay Community Centre is the biggest building. Inside, it looks like a travel agency, filled with brochures and waiting-room chairs. Our school has the same ads for safe sex, but now I learn where to get tested for STDs without anyone finding out. Workers rush from one cubicle to another. A copy machine thumps steadily and churns out paper.

On the bulletin board, the club for gay Chinese (Mandarin-speakers) announces a potluck dinner. Another notice warns people about police raids on Boy Street. That must be the place for money boys, but it is several blocks away from Church Street. The group for parents of gays and lesbians meets throughout the Toronto region.

I should tell Ba to attend. Hah!

I head off to a nearby coffee bar. The cashier grins

in that friendly Canadian way and asks how things are going. I don't answer. My English isn't good enough.

I head to the back and look over the place. The man near me looks like my vice-principal Mr. McKay: broad shoulders, too-tight short-sleeved shirt and hairy forearms. But this man wears a wide-brimmed cowboy hat.

Two women sit side by side holding hands. With their outside hands they clink each other's cup and lift it to the other's lips. They drink again, eyes on each other's faces.

A man with a pink face and stiff white hair bends over a laptop. Earphones plug him into his machine. What's he streaming? Elton John? Madonna? Pairs of men sit at little tables. Two uniformed fellows look like delivery men. A pair in button-down collars and khaki pants could be IT workers, bankers or undercover cops. At the window, a teenager with gray eyes and red cheeks daydreams as he smiles to himself.

If I were a westerner, I'd go and introduce myself. I wonder if he has parents like Ba, or parents like Tyson's.

The men look very serious. I wonder if they'll kiss like straight couples do in public. Maybe it's too early in the day. Maybe these people are just friends. The soft murmur of people talking soothes me.

There's free wireless, so I turn on my computer and check my email. My buddies are looking for me. Kevin asks if I've finally found a girlfriend and am hiding out.

He still thinks I'm straight. Wei claims to have a pirated copy of an advance release of *Red Cliff*, Part Two. Everyone begs to see it. Mila insists that we all vote for the same singers in the All-China Pop Song Award. Kai's mom won four tickets to a Toronto Maple Leafs game. Who wants to go?

Some of my friends would be all right with me being gay. Wei, Kai and Jenny are cool. Problem is, Mila is the queen of our group, and everyone looks up to Jian because he's on the basketball team. I don't know where those two stand. Do I need my friends more than I need to come out?

If people at school knew I was gay, my locker would get smashed and paint would be poured in. I couldn't go anywhere by myself. I'd get beaten up, thrown into a dumpster or chained inside the girls' washroom. Each day I'd walk to school alone and then go home by myself. I may as well be dead. Tyson won't become a friend. His crowd is all westerners, and they never talk to us.

When Mr. Deluca teaches gay rights, students voice loud opinions. They don't do this on any other topic. They say that gay people should be accepted in society but two men shouldn't kiss in public. They say that no one should care who's gay, straight, bisexual or whatever. But in real life, it's different.

I surf in and out of my favorite music and gaming sites. And I Google the new term I learned today, Boy Street.

When I log onto *Rebel State*, wow! I'm a hero! The forum is full of players who support my let's-fight-now stance. They just learned that guerrilla warfare doesn't let them win as much Honor. They're calling for new leaders at Rebel Command. The losers on the other side, all they can do is post a list of guerrilla wars that were won in the off-line world: China, Vietnam, Cuba.

This is the best life, to be on top of the game. I post to the forum. People reply right away, now that they respect what I'm saying. I get on several threads to argue my position. In Chinese, it's much easier than living in English.

I lean back and shut my eyes.

Just for a minute, I tell myself, give them a rest.

A high-pitched squeal jolts me awake. My arm shoots out. I knock the cup to the floor. It shatters.

Where's my laptop?

It's right in front of me.

The cashier comes running.

"Sorry," she says, sweeping up the pieces. Her arm is tattooed with a huge graphic full of color and sharp edges.

Cool!

A fellow worker runs a heavy cord from a mike stand to a loudspeaker.

"It's open mike tonight," the cashier adds. "We have poetry readings every Wednesday night. It fills the place."

Outside it's getting dark. Of course I'm sleepy. I haven't had a good rest in two nights.

I Google "cheap room Toronto" and find a place that charges twenty-five dollars a night for a bed and towel. Better yet, I see on MapQuest that the hostel is close by. I can walk there. That brief nap restored my strength.

I march past office workers heading home and right into the hostel. I don't pause at the door like I did at the shelter. Instead I go straight to the counter and bang the bell.

On a high wooden board, the rules and rates are posted in simple English. It must be designed for the foreigners who travel here. For the lowest rate, I share a room with three other people. The room is small and smells of dirty gym socks, but it looks clean. It overlooks a downtown parking lot. Showers and bathrooms are down the hallway. The staff will take phone messages for guests.

I'd rather hold my head high than take a free bed in the shelter. A warrior always pays his own way.

In the lobby, Japanese and Korean tourists laugh and practice their English. If I stand by them, I'll look like part of their group.

If only I could follow them onto their airplanes and fly back to Asia! Outside, young westerner men loiter at the entrance. They are neatly dressed, trim and alert. They peer up and down the street, as if waiting for someone.

Are they money boys?

At the pay phone in the hostel lobby, I punch in Ma's number. It's early morning in Beijing, but we need to talk. Is she going to send me money or not? That'll depend on what kind of job she has. If she has money, she'll help me out, I'm sure of that. She never hated me the way I hated her during the divorce. How could she? I didn't do anything to cause the break-up. Besides, she's my mother. Of course she loves me. She must.

She answers the phone in a sleepy voice. For a moment, there's something different. She's struggling to sound bright and cheerful. But her voice resumes its weary tone when she learns that it's me.

"Do you know what time it is?" she scolds.

"I wouldn't do this if I didn't have to."

"What have you done? What kind of trouble are you in?"

"I'm living on my own now—"

"Who are you?" a man's voice shouts into my ear.

Who's that, and what's he doing at Ma's place so early?

"I'm her son! I'm calling from Canada."

"She's busy."

"Let me talk to my mother!"

The line goes dead. I punch redial but now the line is busy.

I slump to the wall and let myself sink to the floor.

Ma isn't sending money, and I'm not going to China.

I'm a child again, hearing of events long after they happen. My parents are divorcing? No one tells me until Ma suddenly vanishes and Niang comes to pack my bag and take me to her place. Two years later, we're moving to Canada? No one tells me until the nurse at the hospital complains about the extra paperwork for immigration checkups.

During those two years, Grandfather didn't need to take care of me but he visited. He and Ba stopped arguing. Maybe it was because Grandfather came as a guest to Niang's house or because sometimes she sent a car to bring him over and take him home. But when the topic of Canada came up, Grandfather asked Ba several times if I could stay behind with him even though he lived in a tiny little place. He was so heartbroken that he refused to go to the airport to see me off.

Grandfather was a man of honor. I wish Ma had been more like him.

In one of China's tear-jerking but award-winning movies, a village girl treks to the city to work. The only job she can get is at a massage parlor. She swallows her shame and tells her parents that she's working in a factory. She sends them money regularly. They buy a fridge and a TV and build a new house. They become known for being generous neighbors. When they look for a son-in-law, they get a mountain of offers. People know the daughter sends money home but no one knows how she earns it. She lands a fine husband but her marriage ends when he learns the truth about her.

I'm sure Ma is selling tofu. It's the easiest job she can get. It's like how paper bowls of instant noodles were Ma's best dishes at home. During primary school, if I watched TV instead of doing homework, she joined me on the sofa. If I avoided a school exam by playing sick, she let me stay home.

She told me to work hard at school but she never did the same at the jobs she had. She nagged Ba to stop smoking, but then she bought cigarettes. When we went shopping, she warned me to keep my hands to myself. But at department stores, she tried on lipsticks at makeup counters.

If Ma had been more like Niang, Ba would have stayed with her. Niang uses computer spreadsheets even though she has less schooling than Ma. Her restaurant is thriving and people tell her to run for the Beijing Association's executive. If Ma had one-fifth of Niang's ambition, she'd be rich and I'd be in China right now. Ma would send me to a top school where everyone speaks my mother tongue. All it takes is money.

My stomach growls. I walk through the dusk to Chinatown for a rice box, the cheapest meal around. People who live and shop around here have pinched and guarded faces. They belong to a lower class than the Chinese up north. But without my wallet and bank account, I've become one of them. I eat in a food court, where diners leave hardly any food behind. They slurp at their bowls to drink every drop of soup, suck every string of noodle.

I walk back to the hostel slowly. Where the hell is that father of mine? Has he been phoning my cell, trying to reach me? All he has to say is Sorry and I'll go home. But I won't be glad to go back to school.

It's tough out here. I need a job. But I don't want to work in a restaurant or coffee shop, clearing tables and pouring coffee and smiling at customers all day long. I don't want Ba calling me a loser.

At the hostel, the door to my room hangs open. I pause, frowning. I had locked it. Did my roommates come back?

I run to the bed and reach under the pillow.

My laptop is gone! I pat down the covers. I throw the blankets to the floor. The room spins around me. The door has not been forced.

In a daze, I stumble down the hallway. Some doors are wide open. Guests are propped on floors, lying on beds, plugged into Shuffles and iPods, playing with their laptops.

Their laptops, not mine. I run into the washroom, but it's empty.

At the front desk, I croak, "My laptop is gone!"

The clerk looks up from a paperback and frowns.

Oh, no, I've disturbed his evening.

He repeats my words and sighs, as if the world's dirtiest job just landed on him. He rummages for a pen.

My stomach churns. My MVs and video clips are all gone. So is the backup that I started for my iPod. All my favorite songs, lost. Three years of emails from China are wiped out, along with all my friends' addresses. All the photos of the best times of my life. I'll never track them down again.

That's my entire life! Did I back up my files to the desktop? No.

Now I notice the big sign: *Watch your belongings. Hostel is not liable for lost or missing items.*

The clerk asks me questions to fill out a form. He talks too fast. I don't understand a word he says.

My arm sweeps over the counter. The sign-in book, tourist maps, business cards and a basket of candies crash to the floor. The vase smashes into pieces and water creeps toward the door. A potted plant lands on the ground, too, so black soil suddenly dirties the white tiles.

I pound the counter and scream, "Fuck you! Fuck this stupid hole!"

"Hey!" The clerk grabs the phone. "I'm calling the cops!"

I turn and run. There's no traffic on the road. Dusty shops sell used CDs, junk furniture and second-hand clothes. Thick metal bars protect store windows. Troubled people live here. They could have gotten into my room easily from the window.

I dart around the corner onto a main street and sprint several blocks.

At a park, I fling myself on an empty bench. The playground is still. Homeless people are settled on the benches for the night. Someone plays a harmonica. Others shout at him to shut up. Another man hugs a boom box to his head, but there's too much static to hear the talk show. No one walks the path crisscrossing the park. I bring my feet up and thrust my nose between my knees. My panting is ragged.

My laptop is gone.

My laptop is gone.

I must get back to *Rebel State*. Players are waiting for me to lead the fight against the guerrilla war. Steel's Honor is at stake. You don't offer to lead an army and then back out. The discussions are still going on, and I have to follow the threads. Honor means taking responsibility for your words.

A man strolls into the park humming loudly, pushing a shopping cart loaded with rumpled bags and mashed-up boxes. As they rattle by, the smell of hot coffee and rotting fruit drifts over. He has tied a too-small jacket snugly around his waist with a length of rope. Loose baggy pants are tucked into rubber galoshes that come up his shins. His gray-white hair bounces in a ponytail behind his head. A dog lies atop his belongings, long ears flopping down and sharp little eyes reflecting the lamps.

I must have a laptop. Otherwise I will end up like him.

I need money. Now.

———

I walk slowly to Boy Street. I wait in the shadows where the money boys cannot see me. I have no plan to do anything. I just want to see how things work.

Some men are in pairs, smoking and chatting in low voices. Loners strut in little circles as if thinking deeply or waiting for a friend. Nearby buildings loom dark and silent but the landscaping is neat, with park-like grass and bushes. It's a quieter street with less traffic than the one where I saw the women.

Boy Street runs off from a main road. Traffic is thick, then thin. Thick, then thin. Cars coast by slowly. They pass all the money boys and turn the corner. After a while, they reappear and coast by again. The money boys stay at the curb, under streetlamps. Their tight white shirts shimmer. From cars, men lean out as if they are asking for directions. Sometimes a money boy gets in and they drive off.

It's no big deal, I tell myself. Lots of people use their bodies to make money: athletes and actors and models, even pop singers. All it takes is a nice smile, toned muscles and an open mind. If no one gets hurt, why should anyone care what I do with my body?

I saw a film about three brothers in Beijing. Two of them were money boys. One of them looked like my friend You-peng. As one brother tried to talk his younger brother out of such work, he heard about the job's three advantages: money, freedom and lots of sex.

That's not so bad, is it? Not in China, not in Canada.

This is a family tradition, I can say to people. You know how Chinese families grow rich by making noodles, dyeing textiles or lending money? Well, our family is famous for personal services. Like any other family, we work so that the next generation can live in more comfort than the present one. Isn't that what progress is about? Isn't that how the human race gets ahead?

If Ma does this, then so can I.

I take off my jacket and throw it into the bushes. I lean against a power pole. I'm wearing my new Patterson jeans, freshly washed at the shelter. They were far from cheap and fit well. My sweater hangs loosely from my chest, which I puff out as much as possible. The V-neck shows my white T-shirt, so I should look clean and respectable.

My hands shake from the cold. I shove them into my pockets. If I had known I would be coming here tonight, I would have dropped to the floor and done a hundred push-ups. Was it only two days ago that I used the muscle machine at home?

The money boys have noticed me. I am the only Asian here. They are snickering, waiting to see if I will fall flat on my face. No doubt they know all the ins and outs of this business. Maybe customers who come to Boy Street don't want Chinese. Maybe there is another street for Chinese money boys.

In the Central army, my first sergeant barked out, "Nothing Ever Easy!" while we were training, a motto that we soldiers shouted as we charged into battle.

I'm not bad looking. Nice girls have flirted with me.

In my head, I practice lines of English. I try to hear them in my mind, as they should sound when they leave my mouth.

A car stops. A man calls through the open window, "How ya doin'?"

I freeze. This is far too soon. The money boys are looking at me. I force myself to go closer. I crouch at the door. In the cool night air, the heat of the car jumps at me along with the plush fragrance of the inside. It's too dark to see the driver's face.

The man lets out an impatient breath. "Well?"

I open my mouth, but what falls out is the first line of English I learned: "Good morning, how are you?"

The car jerks away. It stops ahead. A door flies open and one of the money boys jumps in.

I want to leap through the sky to another planet, but I force myself to stand still under the streetlamp. I take a deep breath. My body is shaking. There's no moon, no stars above. Good thing the rain stopped. I hear the faraway swoosh of a jet.

I imagine that in Beijing, people look up and see the same dark canvas. I would give anything to be back at Wangfujing Snack Street, sniffing at the grilled lamb kebabs or crunching through peanuts and greens in a *bao zi*. My buddies and me, laughing and eating under bright lights at night. That would be paradise.

When I land back on the street, another car has stopped up ahead. A young man bends to the window, chats with the driver and then gets in.

A second later the door flies open, and both driver and young man tumble out. They grapple with one another on the sidewalk.

A fight! People are running at me and past me.

"Cops!"

I glance back. One man is putting shiny handcuffs on the other.

Then I'm running, too.

Seven

I stop in front of Rainbow Sushi on Church Street. I want to go in but I don't. I need a safe place but nowhere in the downtown feels right. This afternoon's coffee shop was good but right now it's full of people, packed to the door.

If I walk into this restaurant, the people inside will know that I'm gay. At night diners choose carefully. It's not like stopping somewhere to grab a coffee or to kill time on your laptop. Still, I could pass as a homesick tourist or a relative of the cook — anyone but a kid secretly scouting out the gay world.

The place has the usual decorations: rice-paper screens, mini-curtains and jar-shaped lanterns. It looks more casual than formal. Most of the tables have customers. The mix of people is white, black and brown. No East Asians. That means the food won't be the very best.

"*Irashaimase!*" The host rushes up and bows. He's middle-aged, a bit younger than Ba. A short apron is tied around the hapi jacket that holds in his little paunch. He smiles but looks me up and down as if I am a mirror. His hair is shaved close to the skull, like a monk's.

I nod. I understand the welcome. My friends and I have eaten lots of sushi.

He grunts at me in broken English, "You are Chinese?"

This is another Chinese-run sushi place. I nod. His eyelashes are big and curved, enlarged by mascara.

I want to avoid Chinese people, especially sissy ones like this man, so I turn to go.

"From where?" He speaks Mandarin and grabs my arm.

"Beijing." I shake him off, but then a phrase of music grabs me. It is Sodagreen, the best band in the world! My favorite song, "Little Universe," flashes from the TV screen mounted high in one corner.

Now I have to stay. Qing-feng flies through the air in slow motion. The drums slap me awake, and I want to ride on words that surge with anger and feeling. When the bass player skips rope on stage, I want to jump, too.

Hey, who chooses the music here? The customers don't seem to care that there's Chinese rock music in a Japanese restaurant. The host is too old for Sodagreen.

I look around for the waiters just as one walks up.

One hand grips a water glass and Japanese cup while the other carries a sturdy teapot.

"*Komban-wa*," he says, pouring tea.

"Did you choose the music?" I blurt in Chinese. I'm talking to a waiter. That's something new for me, but this guy is as handsome as Daniel Wu, the Hong Kong movie star.

"You like Sodagreen, too?" He speaks Chinese and his smile widens. "I started following them when they won the Golden Melody Cup."

That means he's a little bit older than me. Good.

"I heard them later," I say, hoping to keep him there. "I didn't follow them until 'Little Universe' came out."

"That was the best year for music!"

A tinny bell rings from the kitchen.

"*Konnichiwa*," he calls out. He gives me a slight bow and smiles an apology before leaving.

I wrap my hands around the hot tea. At first I wanted to eat something light and cheap but now I change my mind. I want to surprise the waiter and catch his attention. I want him to wonder who I am and where I come from. On the menu, the most expensive item is *chirashi* with tuna, yellow tail and salmon. I reach into my pocket and see that I have enough to pay my bill and leave a big tip.

At the next table, the young westerners wear jean jackets and layers of shirts hanging loose like blankets.

Two of them lean back and shove their legs out like brooms. The other two play a game, lining up bottles with different amounts of beer inside and blowing into them to make them a musical instrument.

There are also men with gray hair and no hair, businessmen wearing ties and shiny shoes, jocks in tracksuits, a couple in look-alike sweaters, and a man alone, reading a newspaper.

"Ready to order?"

Rot. It's the host, not the cute waiter. He swings out one hip like an impatient woman.

During the TV coverage of Gay Pride, I walked away when the cameras showed men dressed as women with wigs and makeup. I thought they looked like freaks, as if gay men were really women who were born by mistake into men's bodies. Me, I prefer to look at men's bodies. I've never wanted to wear high heels and lipstick.

I give him my order. He raises an eyebrow, as if wanting to see my money first. Then he grunts, "Good choice. The tuna is very high grade today."

I'm neatly dressed, better than the westerner kids, so he should treat me with respect.

Diners at one table stretch over to the men at the next one. They were strangers a second ago, two separate tables of men each minding their own business.

Suddenly they roar with laughter, the kind of

unstoppable laugh that bends you over to your knees. It makes a solo person feel very lonely and start to worry that nearby people are poking fun at him.

My friends and I make the same racket at lunch. One of us cuts into someone's fashion mistake, or aims a new insult at some innocent fool, and we'll laugh and shove each other around. Other kids walk by and glare at us but we know they're jealous. There's an unwritten law that we'll be noisier and laugh longer if someone we don't like is passing by.

The water glass has a sleek, curvy shape and is light-weight, not plain and heavy like those at our restaurant. Someone around here has better taste than Niang.

A plate of green edamame beans lands on my table.

"On the house," says the cute waiter, grinning.

He's gone before I can say thanks. I grab a bean and suck on the salt.

A window counter connects the dining room to the kitchen. Through the opening I see the host working intently. His eyes are focused on his hands. He wears a pointy paper cap, which makes him look really stupid. He glances up suddenly and sees me. I look away but not before he waves. I don't want him smiling at me.

Where's the cute waiter? Please don't let his shift end. I'll have spent my precious dollars for nothing!

The next Sodagreen song is another favorite: "Oh oh

oh oh." It starts with a catchy Spanish splash, and the graphics are funky surreal art. You're still in this world, but not entirely. The swing in the melody helps me forget this awful day. I want to jump up and dance. There are pumping drums and mashed-up English lyrics. I love the new English word they created: no-kay. It means not okay.

The crash of glass on the floor causes a deathly silence. One of the young westerners caught his foot in a chair while getting up, and he stumbled against the table.

The host-cook rushes from the kitchen wielding a shiny cleaver.

"Uh-oh, uh-oh!" he shouts in English. It sounds worse when he's loud. "You break my glass, you got to pay."

The young man looks at his friends. They shrug at him. He pulls out a ten-dollar bill.

"No problem."

"Not enough!" The host-cook waves his knife. "Pay up! Pay!"

People stop eating. They frown. I want to slide down and hide under the table. That man is an oaf.

"No way!" sputters the customer. "Ten bucks for a glass! It's not enough?"

"No! You got to pay. You got to sing!"

The host-cook pulls a remote from his apron and points it at the TV. On flashes the karaoke menu.

"Pick a song and sing!" he shouts, batting his eyelashes at the diner. "Sing with all your heart! Or I lock the door and you will wash dishes all night!"

He must be the owner.

He shoves out a wireless mike. The young man's friends are grinning. The older men, who must be regulars, start clapping their hands in unison.

The ten-dollar man shakes his head but grins at his friends. He studies the K-menu and clicks the remote. He picks the song from the movie *Ghost*.

Wow! The singer has a deep voice and can actually carry a tune. I can't remember the title, but U2's version is the best.

My cute waiter comes out to watch. I see that other customers glance at him, too. He's a pretty face that brings in customers.

When the singer ends on the long note, the diners applaud. The owner shouts, "No, no, no! Second verse! Second verse!"

What is this, *High School Musical*?

He raises his cleaver again. Now the ten-dollar guy plays along. At the refrain, the owner thrusts an arm around his shoulder and joins in. His tenor voice blends easily with the young man's. I am impressed.

At the end, we give them both a standing ovation. The singers shake hands and the owner hands back the ten dollars. Diners on their way out clap him on his back and promise to come back soon.

This owner knows how to keep customers. Niang could learn a few things from him.

I gulp my water. An empty glass should call the waiter back to my table.

He brings everything all at once: miso soup, sunomono salad and main dish. I was hoping he'd make several trips. I ask for more water and tea. I want to reach out to his forearm and touch the small tattoo shaped like a star. Some of the teams in *Rebel State* wear tattoos, too.

The owner drops into the seat across from me. I frown and wonder how to say "Get lost" politely.

He waves at the TV.

"Do you want to sing?" he asks.

I shake my head.

"I am surnamed Chen." He thrusts one hand over the food.

We shake hands but I keep my name to myself. I keep staring at his eyes, so carefully made up.

"Eat, eat," he cries. "You look hungry! How do you like the rice?"

"It has a nice shine."

"Finally! A customer who appreciates fine cooking. Most westerners eat without looking at the food!"

I drink my soup, tilting the tofu bits into my mouth.

"My wife always said the rice was the most important part of the meal," Chen adds. "I thought it was the meat!"

She must be the one who does his eyes. His fingers are too thick and stubby for such precise work. The wedding band on his finger is sleek and modern. I wonder how he can be gay and dress so sissy and live with a woman. She must be very open-minded.

"Which neighborhood did you live in?" he asks.

"Chao-yang."

"My family lives in Feng-tai."

When I stay quiet, he gets the hint and goes away to clear the tables. Finally I can relax. I look around for the waiter, but don't see him. The restaurant is almost empty now. No more customers came in after me.

The TV monitor shows another Sodagreen MV. I hope that means my waiter is still around.

Chen comes and sits again.

"What a day!" he moans. "Not enough workers. This is no way to run a business."

"Don't Chinese people come here? All my friends eat sushi." It's rude to ask why he can't attract those obvious customers, but it's my way of trying to get rid of him.

"Tonight, they all went to some meeting."

That potluck!

"Were you looking for someone?" he asks.

I shake my head.

"Are you looking for new friends?"

None of his business.

"Your food is not bad," I say.

"No need to be polite," he replies bluntly. "Your face is new. I haven't seen you around before."

He is far too personal.

"Why do you do that?" I ask.

"Do what?"

"Act like a woman." I'm being rude again, hoping to get rid of him.

"Because I sing like a woman!" He puts one hand to his collar and clears his throat. The voice that rings out is the high falsetto of a Chinese opera diva. Easily, he sustains a high note. Then he points to the bar across the street.

"I'm a regular on the stage there, Fridays, Saturdays and Sundays."

The restaurant is empty now. I'm full but pick at the food, hoping to catch another glance of my waiter.

"My mother sings Beijing opera." I mean Niang but it's simpler just to say mother. "Every other week, she invites her friends to practice at our home. I run as far as I can."

"What does your father do?"

"Our family owns a restaurant. We all work there. We serve Chinese food."

"So why are you eating here?"

"Change of scenery."

"I have a son who is your age."

"Is that him working — ?"

"Oh, no! My son is in China. With his mother."

I sip my tea. His wife may not be so open-minded after all.

"Is he doing well?" I ask politely.

"He's smart, so he's not doing badly!" he exclaims. "But China is a mess. Factories are closing. The trains are filled with workers returning to the countryside. There may be mass unrest. The government must change its policies."

"It must be better here for you," I say. "For gay people."

"I do not fear China's police! All you do is pay them off."

"Your life is safer here."

"But my family is in China."

"So why do you stay?"

"People ask my wife and son why our family is not all living together, under one roof. My wife tells people that I went to Canada. Everyone understands that. Everyone thinks I'm a hard worker, a caring provider. If I'm here in Canada, then my wife and son get no further questions. Otherwise, people start to gossip behind their backs."

I put money on the table. When I look up, the waiter is by me, holding the teapot.

"More tea?"

I nod eagerly.

"This is Fung Li-jian." Chen gestures to the waiter. "His English name is Lawrence." He points to me. "I don't know this young man's name."

"My surname is Liu. My English name is Ray." I leap up to shake the waiter's hand.

"This is my Canadian wife," Chen says. "Isn't he beautiful?"

Canadian wife?

"He's a shit disturber." Lawrence grins and rubs his hand on Chen's head. "He thinks he can shock strangers by talking like that. But this is such old news now."

"Then how do you want me to introduce you?" Chen speaks in a lovesick way, like a rich old man talking to his sweet young honey pot.

I drop to my chair with a thud.

I forgot about same-sex marriages. I've wasted my money. The cute guy already has a lover.

Eight

I'm angry and sick to be back at the hostel where I was robbed. But I enjoy my dreams that night. I'm in China, a child, swinging through the air from gymnastic rings. In the big hollow of the hall, I hear coaches shouting and blowing their whistles. I hear the thump of bodies on equipment and mats. The floor rushes at me as I try to move from a back uprise into a handstand.

I hear a shrill whistle blast close by, directed at me. My coach hurries up, shaking his head. Like me, he wears a sleeveless gym shirt and shorts.

"Liu Rui-yong, when you swing, push your heels harder, get them behind you!" he shouts. "Have you not been listening? Watch me!"

We exchange positions and he leaps to the rings. From the floor, I stare at his arm and leg muscles, clenching and rippling. His body is wet from teaching at all the stations. The sharp smell of his sweat thrills me. I want to reach out and touch him. He lands and then boosts me to reach the rings.

I feel warm inside. I see Lawrence's face, not my coach's.

When I get out of bed, I stuff my clothes into my backpack. Without twenty-five dollars for another night here, I'll have to go back to that shelter.

Downstairs, a different clerk is on duty at the counter. It's a woman who smiles at me. I take a deep breath and apologize for making such a mess here last night. Her expression doesn't change. Then I ask her if by some miracle my laptop was found.

Of course it wasn't.

I ask if the hostel will cover my loss.

The clerk shows me the form that I signed during check-in. I already released them from any blame.

Yes, but if a laptop got stolen from a man in a business suit, I bet the manager would be all sorry and helpful, lending him an extra machine and calling the cops to hunt down the thieves.

That laptop held my entire life. All my memory. All my RAM. All my ROM. My entire universe.

I stomp to the door. It's raining. I curse and dig through my backpack to yank out my rain poncho. My clothes are everywhere. Now the clerk joins me on the floor and introduces herself as the manager. She offers me one night's free stay to address my loss. It's hardly enough, but I can't argue, can I?

I take my stuff up and come down again. This time she calls out that I get free pancakes for breakfast. I shake my head.

Why do Canadians stuff their mouths with those soggy lumps of dough? Because of maple syrup. One club at school raised eight hundred dollars selling pancakes in the gym. The immigrant kids stayed away. We'd rather pay to not eat them.

I run through cold rain to the business district, to a coffee bar full of sleek suits and expensive shoes. I shiver while people sip their drinks and study their laptops. It's my turn to pay for a coffee. I reach for my money.

I don't have enough.

I dig through all my pockets, fishing out every piece of loose change. My fingers are stiff but they manage to count the coins. Behind me, office workers clear their throats and rustle their newspapers. At the last moment, I find just enough money.

My last coins go into the cup for tips. Thirty-three cents won't even buy me a phone call.

I sit and look outside. It's raining harder now and a stiff wind drives the drops forward in a slant. They spatter against the glass, sliding like tears on a child's smooth face.

The thunder is an angry drum, echoing high above. People hurry by with newspapers or umbrellas over their heads.

I kill time. The window is cold where I leave my fingerprints. I keep my cup close by to signal that I'm a paying customer with every right to sit and stay. Nobody can kick me out!

The newspapers remind me that I need a laptop so I can read the news in Chinese. The English headlines say a toy factory in China fired seven thousand people. America spent $700 billion on bad banks. World leaders are counting on China to pull Europe out of a global recession.

The planet is in trouble, and so am I. There's a room for me at the hostel tonight but not tomorrow. Jian will probably say no to another loan.

I saw Help Wanted signs in many downtown windows. They were all fast-food places. That's bad. The pay is lousy and I'd have to wear an ugly uniform. Worst of all, customers will look at me and write me off as a loser. But maybe I can eat the food there.

At the first place showing a Help Wanted sign, I ask for a job form. I tell a little lie and claim four years of restaurant experience. I try to print neatly but water drips off my jacket onto the paper and turns the black ink into a smear. When I grab napkins to blot it dry, a woman at the counter watches me with tiny eyes.

I am told to wait.

It's Thursday, so yesterday would have been my night at the restaurant. I wonder who Niang found to fill in for me. Not Jian. His college preparation class is Wednesday nights. That means she had to pay someone.

I need my cell. I'm sure that Niang and Ba have tried to call me. They can't abandon me in the streets like a crippled dog, can they? I want to phone, but I won't beg.

The woman hurries up and introduces herself as the manager.

"So sorry," she says with a fake smile, "but your social insurance number isn't valid. Did you write it down properly?"

"Let me check," I say. Her English has a foreign accent. Will she phone the restaurant for a reference? What if Ba answers? He'd have a good laugh over this. I walk the form toward a table, pretending to reach for my wallet. Then I swerve and scoot out the front door.

Sorry? That woman isn't sorry! She wanted to trap me. Make me look like an illegal immigrant who has no right to be here.

Of course that was a made-up number. What a pain that card was. Niang and I battled over it for weeks. During the time that we lived together in China, she stayed out of my life. I think she was hoping that Jian and I would become friends. She left Ba to fend off my teachers' complaints and to buy clothes for me. Then, after we arrived in Canada, she took charge because she had handled all the immigration details. She nagged me to fill out the forms for a social insurance number.

"You need it to get a job," she reminded me.

"I'm not working," I retorted. "I'm fifteen. I'm a student."

"You need it to open a bank account."

"I don't have Canadian money or savings."

"Bank statements will help prove your residency."

"I'm not staying here."

Annoyed, she told Ba to talk to me. Waste of time. I was even less likely to listen to him.

Months passed. One day she handed me a plastic card. My name was pressed into it in English letters.

"Sign it," she said. "And keep it safe."

She had filled out the application form, signed my name and sent it to the government. Then she went to her bank and opened an account for me, putting in a hundred dollars.

I head to Chinatown, where refugee Chinese and illegal immigrants who can't speak English find dead-end jobs. Their low wages are the reason why food prices in Chinatown are the lowest in all Toronto.

One supermarket has spread its boxes and trays of fruit and vegetables onto the sidewalk. Even as it rains, people are shopping.

I spot a hand-scrawled sign in Chinese. Help Wanted. I ask for the boss. He's a dark wiry man with a garlic bulb nose and hair tinted a reddish golden brown. He looks hideous. He offers me a cigarette instead of his blackened hand. His Chinese is loud. I stand back from him before I get cancer.

"Got work card?" he demands.

"I do, but didn't bring it. Lost it."

"Fah." He blows a lungful of tobacco smoke into my face. "You are a northerner?"

"Beijing."

"Ah, rich people."

"No, not at all."

"You speak Fujian language?"

"No." As if he didn't already know.

"Everyone here speaks Fujian language. They speak Mandarin, too, but mostly Fujian language. If you don't mind, you can work here. It's part-time. Evenings only."

I back off. I need full-time work.

"Let me think about it," I say. I hope the cheap chemicals make his hair fall out in big clumps.

An old man is watching from the bus stop, and I almost run over and hug him. He looks exactly like Grandfather.

Ma used to say that Ba's father had a monkey face: his ears stuck out and his too-large eyeglasses made his bright eyes look bigger. He was a small man with thin, stooped shoulders. This stranger also wears Grandfather's old-fashioned Mao jacket, with two chest pockets and two side pockets, as well as the soft army cap with a big brim and puffy top. Everyone in the family gave Grandfather stylish jackets in wool and nylon, but he only wore his gray Mao jacket and hat.

"All your friends wear new designs," Ma told him once. "Don't you want to fit in with them?"

"What's wrong with being different?" he snapped back.

Above the busy stores that line the street, a big sign in Chinese and English offers immigrant aid, free services in many Chinese dialects, as well as English classes. It's the place that the social worker at the church shelter wanted me to visit. The sign shows the Canadian government's logo, so it must be an honest operation. I go up and tell the receptionist I was sent here from the shelter, but all she does is point at a number dispenser. When I sit, the lady next to me stinks of mothballs.

The waiting room has rows of bright orange plastic seats. The walls are bare, except for ragged red sheets of New Year good wishes that should have been removed months ago. The greasy smells of fresh-cooked food float up from the ground-floor restaurant. Little children cling to harried parents. None of the ancient magazines have covers.

These Chinese wear Chinese brands or fitted jackets tailored from sturdy cloth but in ancient styles. Their feet show the ugly fawn-colored socks that are on sale everywhere in Chinatown. They speak quietly, unlike rich people who want to be heard and noticed by everyone. Their patience with waiting is very dignified.

When my turn comes, I tell the clerk about my wallet and how the homeless shelter sent me here. She gives me a form to fill out. I borrow a pen — the Chinese brand, Hero, which I haven't seen since coming to Canada. By the time I finish my form, a different woman is at the desk so I have to repeat my problem. She says I need to meet with a senior official here, someone who can notarize documents.

"When can I do that?" I ask.

She studies a chart. "Tuesday."

"Next week? I need the documents right away! I'm looking for work."

"Right away?" She gestures behind me. "Each one of those persons wants something right away."

I run down the stairs, making as much noise as I can.

My family never thought much of Chinatown. The first time we came here, I was surprised at how big this district was, full of Chinese restaurants, Chinese stores and Chinese people. I thought, if people want to do Chinese business and buy Chinese groceries, then they should stay in China!

I walk back to Church Street, to Rainbow Sushi. The empty pop can that I kick along the wet sidewalk makes a hollow clatter. I wonder if Chen needs any workers. I'll do any dog-fart job he throws at me: wash dishes, clean the washrooms, wipe down the walk-in cooler. And I hope he doesn't care about a SIN card.

Too bad the handwritten sign on the door says the place is closed every Thursday. Why did Chen choose Thursday? Most restaurants close on Mondays or Tuesdays, the slowest days of the week.

At the main library, I see that some of the public computers aren't being used. No line-ups! Great! Going on line will stop me thinking about my stomach.

The clerk asks for a library card.

"I lost my wallet." That makes me sound stupid, so I add, "It was stolen."

"You want a replacement card?"

"Can I get it right away?"

"Do you have ID?"

"I lost my wallet!" Do adults do this to everyone, or just to immigrant kids like me?

"Well, then sign in as a visitor," she says. "You get half an hour on the machine. There are no extensions. There are no exceptions. If you need more time, you'll have to come back tomorrow."

Yes, sir!

My machine is cold, and I have to try several times before it connects to the server. I can't wait to get onto *Rebel State*. If I won the debate over the war strategy, I could be leading an army!

First I Google Lawrence's name. His face and his little star tattoo are stuck on my mind. But he's not on Facebook. Other people have the same name and a Toronto location on LinkedIn. I guess it's true that Toronto has more Chinese than any other Canadian city. But why is Lawrence hooked up with someone like Chen? I Google Rainbow Sushi in English and in Chinese. No photos of Lawrence. The restaurant doesn't have a website.

On *Rebel State*, my team gives me the latest news. Rebel Command wants us to destroy a fortified signal tower. It receives messages from the ships at sea and sends them inland. This must mean that the guerrilla strategy won. When I check Tally, my Honor is at the same level as before. Rebel Command hasn't deducted anything. Maybe Rebel Command knows that I was right to stand up for the local people. Maybe Rebel Command has been too busy to punish me.

We head up the hill with grappling hooks and ropes. The enemy has laid land traps that we step around or disable. It feels good to be back in action, to have a mission.

Monkey, Long Range and Scholar start climbing. They are halfway up the walls when the tower doors fly open. Attack Wolves charge out. They have always had night sight.

The three of us on the ground fall back. Our friends on the walls are helpless as enemy archers take aim. We shouldn't have sent Long Range up the wall. Now we don't have a sharp shooter on our side.

The screen goes black. My half hour is over.

I slam my fingers against the keyboard. No! The team will accuse me of abandoning them.

I glance at the service counter. My clerk has been replaced by a fellow with long frizzy hair. Maybe the first clerk's shift ended. If I move quickly, maybe I can log back onto the game.

I race around to the entrance and dash to the service counter.

"Can visitors use the computers here?" I ask. "I'm from out of town."

The clerk nods and looks for a password for me. Right at that moment, the female clerk returns.

"All finished?" She smiles at me.

"He wants visitor time," says the male clerk, puzzled. The two workers exchange a glance.

"I told you the rules." The female clerk shakes her head. "Come back tomorrow."

"I didn't check my email," I say. "Can't I have a few more minutes? Not all the computers are being used."

"Sorry, rules are rules."

A young Asian woman standing next to me gives me a sideways look and moves away to make it clear that she's not with me. I curse her silently. I don't want to be connected to her, either. That jacket of hers is the ugliest shade of orange ever invented.

On the lower level of the library, I scan the Beijing newspapers. Not only are they several days late, but the large sheets are hard to turn.

More bad news. Residents fail to stop another *hutong* from being bulldozed for skyscrapers. Two tax collectors are sent to prison for ten years. The police carry out an undercover raid at the train station and fine 120 unlicensed taxi drivers.

China is a tough place. Young people spend their first eighteen years doing nothing but studying for college entrance exams. The pressure is so great that some failed students kill themselves each year. Worse, it's not enough to work hard and get good marks. You need connections to get ahead, to get your foot in the door of the right place.

We all know below-average students will get into good schools with family help. That's why Niang wanted to immigrate. She wanted to give Jian and me a better chance at success. But it's not easy to walk away from the world that you've known all your life and forget all your friends.

While leaving the library, I pass a fire alarm. Nobody is nearby so I give it a quick yank. Bells start pounding right away, and a big voice tells everyone to take the stairs and go outside.

I laugh to myself. I feel like I did a back flip from the rings and landed perfectly with both feet together!

Late in the afternoon, I stand in a bus shelter and watch a crowd of people across the street. They're waiting for the doors to open at the church shelter where I stayed two nights ago.

I don't want anyone to see me. I don't want anyone to think that Chinese immigrants are failures. But if I stand out here too long, the kitchen might run out of food.

When the line shuffles forward, I run over. I pull the hood of my jacket over my head and turn away from the road. Believe it or not, by the door stands a grizzled old man rattling a few coins in a tin can and asking for spare change. To my surprise, people dig into their pockets and give him money!

Inside, the kitchen is serving pizza, which makes the hall smell like our school cafeteria. The cooks are bustling around, dressed in white like real chefs. Maybe they are real chefs. Maybe someone is shooting a reality TV show here. High-school kids are back again, aprons over their jeans and T-shirts. They're beaming and smiling, glad to be helpful, glad to be on the other side of the counter.

My mouth is watering. Just as I get close to the food, I see familiar faces.

Jian and Carla. I turn and rush out.

Then I stop. Maybe this is a chance for me to go home. I'll let Jian drag me back and shout, "Look who I found on the street, begging for food!"

I'm broke. I'm hungry. Without that social insurance card I can't get a job. I need my cell and laptop.

I stare back at the door. But I don't move. If I go home now, Ba will have won.

Later that night, I find myself back on Boy Street. I hope the rain has stopped for good. Even at our restaurant, wet days drag down the business.

The money boys are ready to go. Mr. All Muscles never stands still. His legs bounce up and down as if he's running on the spot. His cycling pants and bike jersey stretch around every curve in his body. Baby-face wears a number 28 hockey jersey and sits atop a newspaper box, tapping at the metal edge between his legs like it's a drum. His head jerks back and forth even though he's not wearing earphones. Maybe he is. The tall skinny fellow with a buzz cut and a blue-jean shirt stretches out and does yoga poses when there are no cars on the road.

I stand by myself. It's cool and I could use my jacket, but money boys don't cover up. They — we — need to show as much body as possible. I pray the cops don't show up.

I feel as though I am in a jerky fast-forward video. Monday I get kicked out of the house. Blippety-blip. Tuesday I am homeless at a shelter. Blippety-blip. Wednesday I dine with a drag queen. Thursday I sell my body. Blippety-blip.

Now that's what I call a good education. I should earn credits for living on the street.

In a movie from China, a gay man from the countryside arrives in the big city. He's cheerful and tells everyone everything about himself, as if rural folk are all innocent and trusting. He meets the editor of a gay magazine. They start living together. Days later, they have sex. Even I know that's fantasy. But I can't help but dream that my first guy will be a nice fellow, gentle and sensitive, and maybe even good-looking.

What a way to lose my virgin status. Go hunt for a stranger on a dark street. Forget dating, forget romance, forget someone cute.

The cars coast by slowly, as if on parade at an auto show. That is strange, because the money boys are the ones on sale. A Mercedes goes by. It is so clean and shiny that it looks new. The boys gaze after it hungrily.

They play with their cellphones, too, which makes my fingers itch. I long for my cell, my iPod, my laptop, my music. The stupidest thoughts cross my mind. If Ba were to drive by and stop, I would jump into his car right away. I should have gone home with Jian.

After a while, I recognize the cars that keep circling. There is a boxy European sedan, a Japanese SUV and a low-hung American sportscar. It's too dark to make out exact models or custom colors. A BMW returns at ten-minute intervals, as if wanting to see all the night's faces before making a final choice.

Then a Lexus stops, and the window slides down.

Nine

"Want a ride?"

The man calls out in Chinese. A fellow countryman. Speaking Chinese will speed up things.

I pull the door open and hop in. The man has a tired, middle-aged face. His glasses are sleek black rectangles that have arms etched with thin gray lines. In the dark, I can only see an outline of his hair, but it seems thick, pulled up in short little spikes.

This man is trying hard to look younger. His car reeks of cigarettes.

"What's your name?"

"Ray."

"Real name?"

"Yes." Rot. Forgot to lie. Ah, not to worry. English names don't matter.

"I am surnamed Han."

He reaches over and we shake hands. His palm is warm. Mine is icy cold.

The money boys are looking at us. They must be annoyed that a Lexus man picked me. I want to sail by them.

"Are we going?" I demand.

"Of course. Of course."

But the car doesn't move. The man frowns at me, as if trying to recall my face from somewhere. Is he a cop? Maybe I should run. Then the money boys on the sidewalk would stamp their feet and hoot with laughter, watching me tumble out of the car so quickly.

Loser!

"What's the matter?" I demand.

"This . . . this isn't your first time, is it?" he asks.

"Of course not." I act insulted and grab the door handle. "Shall I leave?"

He shifts gears, the car lurches, and we swerve into traffic on the main road. Bars of golden streetlamp light pass over his face. He's better than average looking, almost handsome with a lean nose and thick eyebrows. Too bad he's so old.

He runs through a red light and rumbles over streetcar tracks. At a bank, a sign blinks out the time and temperature and stock market prices. It's almost nine p.m.

How long will this take? How much can I earn in an hour?

"Where to?" I try to sound bored.

He exclaims, "Hey, you know what?" as if a wonderful idea just popped into his head. "I need to eat something first. Do you mind? Join me?"

"I ate." I lie because I want to get this over quickly. But I'm hungry, too.

"My treat."

"Can't we keep this simple?" I don't want him in control of everything.

"Ah, young people today are always in such a hurry."

He thinks he's funny!

"Time is money," I declare. That line would make Ba proud.

"Yes, yes." He nods agreeably. "So, tell me. How many clients will you get tonight?"

"How would I know? I'm not a fortune-teller." I talk as if I'm with Ba, so every word is surly and rude.

"It's Thursday. The middle of the week can be slow. Not many cars were going through your street."

He sounds like an old hand. I want to know about the pay. How many nights of rent can I make from one job?

"Decided yet?" he asks. "Eat or not?"

"Do as you want." I stare glumly out my window.

He pulls a sharp turn. We head west. I look for landmarks that might guide me back to the downtown.

These streets, I haven't seen them before. It's an old part of Toronto, with bumpy streetcar tracks underfoot and darkened shops behind heavy metal grates. They stand between lonely cafés lit by beer-logo neon and milk stores under big flat signs. People walk quickly, heads down, as if afraid to see too much.

Where are we going? Niagara Falls? Buffalo? How will I get home? Maybe now's the time to jump out.

Then, something deep inside me gives way. The balloons of my lungs lose their air and collapse. My chest shudders.

I'm too tired to care anymore. I've been alert every single minute of the day: watching and waiting, hoping and pushing, trying this and trying that. Nothing has worked out and yet my entire life seems to lead up to this moment.

I want gay sex.

It will prove things.

It'll be the one reward for this week of dog farts. I just hope this guy Han can be trusted.

At a Vietnamese restaurant, strings of Christmas lights frame the front window. Overhead, a neon sign glows green, red and yellow, all the good-luck colors. Han digs into his pants for coins to plug into the parking machine. His designer jeans fit him tightly.

I shiver on the cold street and glance from side to side, looking for a street name. Nothing.

Relax, I tell myself. If this guy is a madman, he wouldn't be paying the meter, right?

Eager waiters wearing green vests greet him by name and address him in Cantonese. I don't understand and I don't care. His surname really is Han, unless he uses many names.

Business isn't bad for so late at night. The place has two young-looking couples. A table of seven or eight older men is noisy. They wear boiler suits and dirty T-shirts. They probably just got off work from a garage or factory. Beer bottles crowd the tablecloth. One of their buddies shouts as he rejoins them. He was puffing on a cigarette as fast as he could outside the front door.

Han orders without the menu and calls for a Japanese beer. I'm thirsty, too, but don't want to make trouble. I'm eighteen but still too young to drink here. Coke for me.

Han raises his bottle and we toast each other, aluminum can slapping glass bottle. My eyes avoid his. This feels like a cheap movie about hookers. My minor role is stuck with tired lines recycled from old scripts.

"Been doing this for long?" He smiles. His teeth seem strong and healthy.

"A while."

"I haven't seen you before."

"I haven't seen *you* before."

His head dips slightly. "That's our misfortune, then,"

he says. "You're handsome. You take good care of your body. That's smart of you."

Smooth as a salesman selling lightbulbs to blind people, isn't he? The mirrored bar at the back is stacked high with liquor bottles and statues of Chinese gods. More colored lights dangle over them. Niang would redecorate this place in a flash.

Will we do the deed in the washroom? Is that why we came here, to where people know him, to where people will look the other way and not disturb us?

"Looks like you watch over your body, too." Then I add, "My father is overweight, like a government official."

He frowns. His face darkens. I knew that mentioning my father would do that.

"Your father," he says after a long chug of beer, "does he live here or in China?"

The food arrives all at the same time amidst a clatter of large platters. I start slowly, picking at the food, watching him and chewing carefully. The food is piping hot and tasty. He ordered seafood soup, curried chicken, grilled beef in rice paper, and crispy shrimp with black pepper vegetables. There are several sauces for dipping.

When I finally put down my chopsticks, I burp loudly from eating too fast. Not a scrap of food is left. I told myself to go slowly, but my stomach took charge.

In *Rebel State*, some commanders send hungry soldiers

into battle, thinking they will fight harder in order to quickly get to food. Other commanders feed their soldiers first, worried that hungry soldiers are weaker and will be defeated quickly. Me, I eat every chance I get.

Of course Han saw how quickly I ate. Now he knows I'm hungry. That gives him power over me. Not good.

"The usual rate?" I ask, trying to sound cool. "For tonight."

"Of course."

If only I knew how much that was.

He's decent and generous to feed me. He seems quiet and thoughtful. He doesn't talk my ear off. His hands are big and strong. He dresses young.

A flicker of eagerness glows in my gut. I'm warmed up for the big scene in a steamy movie. I want him. I pray for this evening to succeed. He's paying money, and every customer should be satisfied.

He calls for the bill politely. At our restaurant, some diners raise their hands and snap their fingers.

He twiddles a toothpick between his teeth, just like Ba.

My heart is pounding loudly.

"You know," he says, "you might be able to do me a big favor."

"What?" My voice squeaks. I sit on my hands. Good thing he can't see such a childish move.

"No." He shakes his head at himself. "Too embarrassing."

It sounds so stupid that I snort, "Is it really that bad?"

"Yes."

"What is it?"

He looks away and mumbles like a child. "I want to go bowling."

I burst out laughing. I can't help myself. It's been a long time since I had a good laugh.

"I have no friends who bowl," he says. "Before, I played all the time. I miss it."

"How do you know I do bowling?"

"All young people bowl."

"Will you pay more?"

"If you win, then I'll pay an extra forty dollars."

"And if you win?"

"Then we're even."

"You're generous."

"More people ought to be generous," he declares. "It's good for the soul."

The bowling alley is somewhere midtown, reached through long roads lined with low-rise apartment blocks. It's dark and quiet, but a solitary man is out walking a little dog. Its tiny legs are a blur, darting ahead of the leash.

First a free meal and now bowling. The movie that

I'm in is turning into an art film that doesn't make sense. But on a full stomach, I'm lazy. If Han keeps paying my way, he can do whatever he wants.

After we arrive, I see trouble. Han likes to win. Not only was he carrying his own shoes and ball in the trunk of his car, but he also flips a coin to start. He wins the toss and gets a strike on his first throw. He grins and punches the air like a star athlete.

What a dog-fart show-off.

I manage some spares. Forty dollars is a lot of money. I need to hook the ball, but I can't remember how to do it. I'm too nervous.

Every throw Han makes is smooth and certain. Nothing goes down the gutter.

Han yanks off his pullover. A tight black T-shirt outlines his meaty chest and arms. It's clear this man works out. When he runs to the line and stretches to make his throw, the fabric across his haunch tightens.

In the second game, I get better. But it's no fun playing catch-up to someone who likes winning more than having fun. He doesn't buy pop or chips. He doesn't laugh or horse around. He doesn't try to cheat on the score pad like my friends do. He's so boring!

Then I remember to aim for the arrows.

A strike!

Han notices. He claps lazily. From then on we're better

matched. I win two games out of five, and our scores are close.

He grabs his bag.

"How about two more games?" I say. "I can beat you."

He shakes his head.

"Afraid to lose?" I ask.

"Exactly," he says. "This way I keep my money. Let's go."

"Where?"

"My place."

We take the freeway south, toward the downtown. Far in the distance are the lights of the CN Tower, glowing like some alien spaceship. I'm ready to blast off on a big trip. I let my body fill the smooth curve of the deluxe leather seat. I squint at the silvery rainbow of CDs above the windshield. Probably classical music.

"Working on the street," he says, "doesn't it scare you?"

"All cities are dangerous."

"Hooligans go to Boy Street, surround a money boy and beat him until he vomits blood."

"Are you worried about me?" I ask.

"Of course I am."

"I can take care of myself."

"I can take care of you, too."

Is he flirting with me? I keep my mouth shut.

After a while he asks about my hobbies, my free time.

"Have you heard of *Rebel State*?" I ask. "It's an on-line role-play game."

He shakes his head.

"Did you ever play computer games?" I ask. Han talks like an educated man. He must know computers.

"*Great Wall Northern Defense.*"

"That was a long time ago!"

"I hear the technology is much advanced now."

I fold my arms over my chest and stare at the road.

Why bother to update this old fart? I don't care to make small talk. He's too old for games, anyway.

We drive into a brightly lit underground parking lot and then ride a quiet elevator that climbs forever. The numbers above the door blink their way up to 30. Han whistles a Cantopop melody. I hate Cantopop.

When the door opens, I stumble over a soft carpet. Han disables the burglar alarm and says, "There's not much space here."

Liar. Floor-to-ceiling windows stretch along an entire wall. We're floating above the city. Around me, rows and rows of windows, lit and unlit, form arcs of oblong eyes, all staring at me. Business logos blink atop the towers. Rain taps gently on the window.

Gallery lamps here and there — on the walls and in the cabinets — perch over paintings and statues to light them properly. Gleaming hardwood floors are covered with silk carpets. The deep red walls match his cushions and lampshades.

This is not a typical immigrant home, which has no furniture except for a mah-jongg table and a wide-screen TV.

How long has he lived in Canada? And how does he earn his money?

I excuse myself. The bathroom is a temple for worshipping a framed poster of a naked man. His perfect westerner's body is big and beefy. He stands among cowboy props and shadows that hide his private parts. The bathroom's wall-to-wall mirrors let me see myself, too.

I don't look half bad, even next to the poster fellow. I have muscles in the right places, my face has even features, and my skin is smooth with good health.

Han is in the little kitchen, at a hot-water dispenser. The sound of water spurting out takes me far away for a second. Popo always had the latest model and rushed to serve hot drinks to visitors to show it off.

He hands me a mug of hot water.

"Can we start?" I say. "I need to get back to work."

"It's raining." He sips his water slowly. "You should take a night off."

Does he want me to stay longer? Will he pay more?

He goes to the living room, to one of two white leather sofas, each long enough for a man to stretch out full-length.

"This is your first time, isn't it?" He leans back and drops his feet onto a huge glass coffee table. "You're new to all this, aren't you?"

"So what?"

"Go slowly. You're young. You've got your whole life ahead of you."

"You don't want to pay me?"

Han promptly counts out some twenty-dollar bills.

"I've got to do this!" I say. "I'm no beggar."

"I know."

"This is business," I insist.

"I have a favor to ask."

Again?

Han's fingers rub at his forehead, as if he's got a headache. Then his hand shoots up and all his hair lifts off.

He's bald. The overhead lights gleam on his shiny crown. I never knew you could get wigs that looked so young and hip.

Han looks older than Ba. I look away to his shelves of books. There are English and Chinese titles. The wall holds a long scroll with gigantic Chinese brushwork on it.

What's this old man trying to prove?

"I want to lie down with you," he says, "and hold you in my arms. We would keep our clothes on. But I don't want to wear this fake hair."

"Let's do it." I'm keen to start.

"Are you sure?"

He reaches out and pulls me to the sofa. The leather is soft and warm, but I'm stiff and awkward as a board.

"Drink some hot water," Han says. "Relax."

"I'm fine." I shrug my shoulders to loosen them. I gulp the hot water and let its warmth tingle inside me.

Han aims a remote at the TV. A basketball game comes on and he mutes the crowd noise.

"Watch the game," he whispers. "Pretend you are at home with your family."

I lie on my side. Han hovers behind me. He gently pulls me against him, and then his hands wander over my upper body, rubbing small circles into my chest and arms. The tobacco odor on him is strong. It reminds me of Ba and makes me choke on a breath.

"Relax," he says again. "You can enjoy this, if you want."

His lips and chin nudge my ears and neck. There is fresh mouthwash on his breath.

What a gentleman, I tell myself. What a thoughtful man. I tremble, and keep my eyes on the action on the TV screen. Han wriggles closer and the solid muscles of his chest and thighs press into me. He is an old man, but he is in better shape than me. His breathing is hot at my back, and his entire body is warm.

I fold myself into him. It feels fine.

Ten

When I awake, it is late afternoon. Of course I slept in. I didn't get back to the hostel until dawn.

My bonus free night at the hostel turned out to be a room to myself. What a treat. What perfect timing.

I congratulate myself. I'm not a virgin anymore! I'm all grown up now.

I relive last night over and over, moment by moment. Han and I, we feasted over a Vietnamese meal. We competed fiercely at the bowling alley. He trusted me enough to take off his wig!

Last night confirms it. I'm gay. I roll the words over my tongue, in English and in Chinese.

Homosexual.

Wo shi tong xing lian de.

I want to shout this out to Ba and Niang, Wei and Kai, Jian and Carla, Mila and Jenny. Now I'm the man

I'm supposed to be.

My stomach rumbles. I throw on my clothes from yesterday, sniffing at them for traces of Han. Then I hurry up Church Street to the coffee bar. The sky is bright blue. A biting wind whips down from the north, but I hardly feel the cold.

The coffee bar is warm with rich smells of fresh coffee and baking sugar. I'm starved, so all the food looks good. I choose Italian biscotti, Danish pastries, English scones and Swiss chocolate cake. The clerk loading up my tray smiles.

"So good to see someone with an appetite!" she exclaims. "Most of our customers eat too carefully."

"I'm very hungry," I tell her.

Walking to my table, I see that most customers buy only one piece of food. They dip a biscuit into their drink or nibble slowly on a muffin. They look very serious.

I want to raise my espresso cup and shout to everyone, "Hey, look around! It's a beautiful day!"

I check the newspaper for today's date so I can carve it into my brain. Of course this is a big deal, doing the deed and doing it safely. I look up and grin at people passing by. No one returns the smile.

It's frustrating to have good news without anyone to tell. When Jenny got her driver's license, she texted us and we all met at the mall in half an hour. When Kai learned that he would be spending the summer in China, we got so giddy that it felt as if everyone was going.

So what do I say?

I'm gay. Ba found out and kicked me out of the house. I lost my ID and my cell and then my laptop. But I met new people downtown, very different people. Out there, it's easier to be your own person.

Yeah, I sell my body for sex. It's no big deal. We all need money, the more the better. We all want sex, the sooner the better.

I'll tell them that I wasn't sure. I'll say that the only way to be a hundred percent was to try gay sex. I can't admit being too afraid to come out. They'll laugh and accuse me of being old-fashioned. I'll tell them how great it was to see another human body get turned on the same way as mine. They'll never know how exciting a man's body is. It's all beautiful. I want more and don't want to hide myself.

My fingers itch to flick open a cell and start texting. They must be out of shape from lack of use. Better do warmups and exercises. Maybe full-body pushups on my fingertips?

I want to add jokes and funny details to my story, to make my friends laugh. It's up to me to show them that I like things this way. If they don't accept me, then it's too bad for them. I'll find new friends in the gay world, like Han.

Wait. Can I still be in the gang if I don't see my friends every day in class? Am I going back to school?

Don't worry about school. That means going home and facing Ba. That's a dead end.

I hate how all this gloomy stuff squashes my good feelings. Rot that dog-fart father of mine!

I can't sit still. I'm still hungry so I go to Rainbow Sushi. Now I have enough money to eat chirashi every day. And I can watch that Lawrence. Too bad he's married already. I guess that's another reason for me to come out now. Soon all the good-looking men will be taken.

On the door of Rainbow Sushi, a sign announces *Friday Afternoon Song Time, All Welcome.*

Inside, I get slammed to the wall by "Big Ocean," the howling love song from Taiwan. A portable keyboard sits by the loudspeaker. On the TV, the singer sings with his entire body.

When my friends and I go to a K-bar, we do the same. Crouch from the knees, fill the gut with power and then belt out notes like baseball players hitting home runs.

The crowd is a mix of Asian men, all ages. Some are in business dress. That startles me until I tell myself that I lost a day but found a new life. Chen hands out cold beer as he comes toward me.

"Wah! You look good!" he trills in Chinese. He gives

me a squishy hug. "Is it the daytime sunlight, or have you met someone special?"

I pull back. His sissy manners make me wish I had gone somewhere else. But the music here is perfect.

"Do you sing?" Chen asks. "Or play the piano?"

"I have no talent." I gesture at the crowd. "You are wise. You draw afternoon customers and fill up the slow time."

"People want a comfortable place where they can have fun."

"Does everyone perform?" I ask.

"Of course! And everyone wants to see your fresh face!" Chen heads off but spins around. "Hey, the other night, I meant to ask you if you were looking for work. We always need extra help."

But now I can make much more money on Boy Street.

"Of course you have plans already!" He grins at my hesitation. "Just give me your telephone number, in case of an emergency."

I give him the hostel's phone number and an order for sushi.

"Want me to introduce you to people?" he asks. "The younger ones are here today."

"How about I eat first?"

Young strangers are frightening. Chen was easy. He parked himself at my table and tank-rolled into my life.

Han and I, we did business so that proved easy, too. Besides, Chen and Han are older and know how to chat. Younger men laughing in a circle, they're a fortress with no door. A stranger can walk around them and around them and never find an opening. It's safer to sit back and act bored.

The karaoke machine makes raindrop sounds. "Family Too Far" is a tough song to sing, with high soaring notes and fast and slow lines. Its original singer moved to Canada before Hong Kong was returned to China. When I lived in Beijing, I didn't respect stars who abandoned the homeland. Now I'm here in Canada, while he's gone back to China.

The chorus lyrics are strong yet touching: *We have no family, our name is orphan, going home is a call inside a dream.* There is anger and then soft dreams and love. The words are bittersweet but the melody lifts us.

The audience gets teary-eyed and everyone sings the refrain. I join in, too, under my breath.

Lawrence greets me with my food. "Your name is Ray, isn't that so?"

He remembered my name! I nod eagerly. He's not dressed for work today. Instead, a button-down collar shirt and Dockers give him the smooth look of the well educated. He looks like what every Chinese mother wants her son to become.

"Are you singing?" I ask.

Before he can reply, Chen calls him away. At the front, they pick up mikes. The audience hoots and makes catcalls.

"No costumes?"

"Show some skin!"

"Bring on the dancers!"

They perform an English-language song. Chen and Lawrence talk their way into it. They each sing single lines. During pauses, the other one does background yeah-yeah-yeah's or no-no-no's. Their voices harmonize. Their gazes meet. They hug each other and hit the high notes together. Everyone cheers.

The song has a catchy beat. One minute Chen and Lawrence croon to one another like lovers in a tight duet. Next minute they throw their arms out to plead with the crowd. Their voices meld into one. People shout for more.

What a show! I jump up and clap, hands above my head. Lawrence and Chen kiss each other on the lips and bow to the crowd.

They bring wet beers to sit with me. They are catching their breaths.

"I'm your fan forever!" I exclaim. "I never saw men sing like that!"

"Copied it from Hollywood," Lawrence says.

"A movie about karaoke, in America," Chen adds.

"We watched it tens of thousands of times."

"You two should enter contests," I declare. "You'd win for sure!"

"No, thanks." Lawrence shakes his head.

"Do you like restaurant work?" I sound like an old man to ask that question but I can't be shy anymore. This is the start of a new life!

He shrugs. "I was a banker until I got laid off."

"Banker?" I never would have guessed.

"My MBA is from Harvard," he adds proudly. "So this is just a temporary situation."

"He wants to return to China," says Chen.

"That would be great," I say.

"And he will not go," Lawrence interrupts, pointing at his partner.

"How can he?" I recall details from two days ago. "His family lives there."

"We can disappear into any city in China. His wife would never find us," Lawrence declares. "Truth is, he has fallen in love with Canada!"

"Hah!" Chen makes a sour face. "This one says that as long as we make lots of money, we will be happy in China."

"And *he* says he must live openly as a gay man," Lawrence retorts, "otherwise he says he will be miserable."

"No one has rights there!" Chen says. "We will never have any freedom."

"If we have money, people will leave us alone. Who cares about human rights?"

"I do."

"I should never have married you," he jokes.

"What will you do?" I ask. Lawrence is young and good-looking. He has a future to look forward to!

"Fight to the death!" they chime together.

A hand lands on my shoulder. I turn around.

It's my father. He wears his black leather jacket and looks like a cop.

"Rui-yong," he says, "time to go."

He's the last person in the world I want to see.

Chen sticks his hand out to shake.

"Come, have a seat," he says to Ba, gesturing to a table.

Ba squints at Chen's eye makeup. He doesn't offer his hand. Lawrence notices and frowns.

I throw one arm around Chen and pull him close, as if he's my closest friend.

"This is Old Chen," I tell Ba. "He's from Beijing, too. He helped me out." And I say to Chen, "This is my father."

"Good to meet you!" Chen exclaims, ignoring Ba's insult.

"And this is Fung Li-jian, or Lawrence," I say. "He's a banker. He has an MBA from Harvard. He is Old Chen's wife!"

Without a word to my friends, Ba drags me away to the corner near the front door.

"I said, let's go," he says. His gaze is fixed on me, as if he's afraid to look around this place.

"You kicked me out," I retort. "You don't want me."

"I'm your father."

He has visited the barber since last week. Barbs of white stick out of his crew cut.

"Five days have gone by!" I sputter.

"You wouldn't answer your cell," he says accusingly.

"I got robbed!"

"I walked up and down this street yesterday. I went into every store. I got wet as a chicken in soup." He pulls my arm. "Let's go home."

The word "home" tugs at my heart, but I'm still angry. Chen and Lawrence peer over at us.

"I've changed," I declare. "I'm a different person now. You don't know me."

Ba stares blankly at me, waiting.

Finally I say, "If I go home, then what?"

"Go back to school. Study hard to enter college. Make your grandfather and your mother proud. You'll stop visiting those gay sites. And never talk about gay matters again."

I explode into little pieces. My hands fly up. They almost grab his throat and squeeze.

The front door opens, and Han walks in.

"Ba, you better go," I say.

"Take some money." Ba reaches for me but I fling him off.

I want to rush to Han, throw my arms around him and pull his solid body into mine. But I'm not as brave as I thought, not with Ba standing there.

"Ray, you're here, too!" Han exclaims.

"What's up?" I ask cheerfully.

"Came to sing, to relax. Just like you."

Ba barges in and shoves Han away.

"Leave him alone," he hisses.

"Don't push!" Han shoves back. "I'm his friend. Who are you?"

"My son does not need friends such as you."

Han glances at me. "What do you want, Ray?"

"Let me run my own life!" I shout.

Ba curses me loudly, and then dashes out the door.

Lawrence pulls me to the booth, to my sushi.

"Don't pay your father any attention," he says. "You're old enough to decide for yourself."

Chen brings me a can of Coke. I pour it down my throat to wash away the bad taste in my mouth

The younger crowd moves away from the K-machine to surround Han. They call his name and kiss and hug him. The older men hang back and chat among themselves. They seem wary of Han, watching him with guarded eyes. The crowd breaks into two noisy clusters.

Chen brings over the young men and introduces them. They tell me their surnames and where in China they come from, but the details don't stick in my mind. They ask how long I've been in Canada, what kind of work I do, and where the best Beijing food can be found in Toronto. I tell them about Niang's restaurant. I try to find out if these men live nearby or in the immigrant suburbs. Ba made me lose my appetite, so I'm happy to share my sushi with these new faces.

Han interrupts and pulls me away. I offer him some sushi.

"I have business to tend to," he says, holding up his cell. "How about we meet tomorrow?"

"Sure!" He wants to see me again! He's not bothered by Ba's rudeness. I knew he wouldn't be. He's too cool.

At the keyboard, someone is playing "I Believe." The song is upbeat. People are dancing. It is one of the few Chinese songs without the sappy romantic stuff about love and loss. In fact, Lawrence resembles one of the actors in the MV version, all successful and high-fiving his colleagues. Someone grabs the mike and I join him. I dance, too, closing my eyes to let my body find the music.

I shake my head hard, trying to escape the gloom that Ba threw onto me.

I made Ba lose face in front of my new friends. Ba will hate me forever. I doubt that I'll ever see him again. We're finished. Our family is finished.

Then I'm singing the words on the screen.

Believe in me and tomorrow is yours,
Believe in youth and the energy roars.

When I rejoin the crowd, Lawrence gives me a big hug.

"You should sing more often. You have a good voice!"

In our family, Ba claims to have the best voice for karaoke.

Then Old Chen nudges me.

"You met Mr. Han, have you?"

"Just yesterday."

"Stay away from him. He's a pimp."

I don't miss a beat.

"I know," I declare. "I met him on Boy Street. How do you think we became acquainted?"

Chen and Lawrence glance at one other.

"Don't go to him again," says Chen. "His kind of money comes easily, but there are better ways to live."

"You're young," says Lawrence. "Your life is just starting. Go home with your father."

They're all the same, these old men, trying to squash the energies of young people. I feel sorry for them.

"This was great!" I gesture at the karaoke machine and keyboard. I give them cheerful goodbyes, pretending not to be bothered.

"You haven't finished your sushi!" Chen exclaims.

I'm already out the door.

I'm the world's biggest fool.

Only an idiot presumes that an elegant big-shot such as Mr. Han might be interested in an immigrant nobody called Ray.

Han owns fine artwork and has a great body. He knows gay life in Toronto backwards and forwards.

Less than a week ago, I was hiding in the closet afraid of being gay.

I thought that Han liked me, enjoyed my company and wanted to be a friend!

I was so happy to give myself to him! He was gentle. He patiently explained things. He told me over and over how handsome I was.

Instead I was being led around like a toddler taking his very first steps. He was checking me out, to see if I would fit into his business. I was nothing to him but another body on Boy Street.

Eleven

Internet cafés are costly and hard to find now that everyone owns a laptop.

After leaving yesterday's K-party at Rainbow Sushi, I went to a basement shop for on-line gamers and bought a block of computer time. It was cheaper that way.

But as soon as I logged on, I wanted to leave. The stink of old pot and cigarette stubs was strong. The brown carpet of wormy fibers on the floor was sure to be infested with bugs and parasites.

The war was going badly. We lost Monkey and Long Range during Thursday's botched raid on the signal tower. Central punished the local people for helping Heaven Hand and Scholar to escape. Its soldiers marched into three villages and took thirty slaves.

Yesterday we ambushed the slave convoy. But enemy soldiers were hidden among them, dressed as slaves.

When their chains were removed, they pulled out hidden weapons. In the fight, Heaven Hand was captured. That means I have to log back on this morning.

But scrolling through *Rebel State*, I keep thinking about Han. Should I meet him for lunch? Do I want to work for him? If I don't, what will I do for money?

The enemy ties Heaven Hand to a post. They pour sweet wine over him, luring insects to eat him alive. They challenge us to send a warrior to fight the Sentry who guards Heaven Hand. If our fighter wins, then Heaven Hand will be set free. If our fighter loses, then both rebels will die.

I'm leader of Heaven Hand's team, so it's my duty to fight. The Sentry wears heavy armor. I dance around him, but he is stronger and tosses me around like a toy. His spear keeps me away. Finally I get close by rolling through like a runaway log. With both my hands, I swing my sword and break his spear. Soon I have one foot pressing him to the ground. I use my sword to open his visor.

The Sentry is a woman! An old hag with white hair and leathery skin spits at me. I protect my face against her poisoned saliva.

To kill a woman will reduce my Honor. But I have no choice. It's my duty to save Heaven Hand.

So I do.

I don't like being caught off balance. I'm supposed to be in control here. After Heaven Hand is set free, I log off without joining the victory celebration.

Instead, I count my real-world money. I paid rent last night, and will need to do so again today. Yesterday it felt smart to refuse Ba's offer, but now I'm short of cash. I still need a cell and laptop.

I've got no choice but to meet Han and make a deal with him.

———

He takes me to a little Italian restaurant where the inside walls are brickwork just like the outside, only cleaner. I guess diners are supposed to imagine that they're eating outside in the fresh air, in some warm southern climate.

The menu is written in Italian, in fancy script. I can't read the words, and no doubt Han is waiting to see me make a fool of myself. Why else did he choose this place?

"This restaurant is one of Toronto's best," he says.

I stare at his hair. It's a wig and he's an old man, I tell myself. I'm young and he's not.

"Will you order now, gentlemen?"

The waiter drapes the cloth napkin over my lap and arches a bushy white eyebrow at me.

I gesture to Han. "He goes first."

I duck behind the tall boards of the menu. Han's

English is free of an accent. He's lived here a long time. Or he had really good teachers. Maybe his family in China has lots of money. He jokes with the waiter, an old man who seems puzzled by how much Han knows about wines.

The waiter turns to me. I raise my glass of water and say loudly, in my best English, "I will have the same as my father."

Han chokes and sprays out a mouthful of water.

I laugh out loud.

The waiter withdraws quickly and quietly. I switch back to Chinese.

"What were you saying about good restaurants?"

Han uses a napkin to dab at the water on his shirt.

"You know, you never asked about my line of work."

"I know what you do." I make myself sound bored.

"You're very clever!" He flatters me like an adoring grandparent. "Who told you?"

"People. At Rainbow Sushi."

"Old Chen and Lawrence?"

I nod.

"Then I'm surprised you showed up today."

"Why? I know what you want!"

"So we know what I want." He pauses. "But I don't know what you want."

"I need a laptop. You know I play on-line games. I need to stay on top of things."

"What? Did your head get slammed in a door?" He shakes his head. "You're here because of a computer game?"

I shrug. The waiter presents him with a bottle of wine, opens it and lets him sniff the cork.

Yeah, I'm a stupid kid. And I don't mind if Han believes that. This is all about survival, about paying the rent.

"The food here is famous," Han says. "You know, every time we meet, you have food in front of you. You're still a growing lad."

"You pimp," I say in Chinese. *La-pi-tiao* is an insult.

"Want some advice?" he asks. "Go home and go back to school."

"Want some advice?" I say. "Change the subject."

I want to stomp out, but I'm hungry. Every meal is important. I take a breath.

"Tell me, how did you start in this . . . line of work?"

Han sips his wine and glares at me. I can't tell if he likes my question or not.

"I came here a long time ago," he says. "My job brought me downtown and to Church Street. I'm a computer expert. Everyone needed me. I met lots of people."

Slept with lots of people, I think. You must have had great fun. You were young. You were good-looking. You had all the luck in the world.

Now he's bragging, and I regret asking.

"The men I knew, they knew more people. I knew many Chinese immigrants, and I knew many westerners. Some of my westerner friends really liked Chinese men. But they had no way to meet them. They asked me to introduce them to my Chinese friends. Now I provide a service, connecting westerners to Chinese men. It's a dating service. Will you work for me?"

Do I have a choice? Do I want to stand outside in the cold, watching cars with heated leather seats coast by? Do I want to be looking out for the cops all the time? Han can make my life much easier. Every customer will be someone who wants a Chinese boy.

I play hard to get. "Why should I work for you?"

"Safer," Han declares.

"I take care of myself," I retort. "My father was an army instructor. He taught me how to fight."

"You get high-class clients who will treat you gently and with respect."

"Good," I say. "Immigrants get little respect these days. What else?"

"You'll earn money. Yesterday you were begging. You were starving to death."

"Chen offered me a job at Rainbow Sushi. I can work there."

"For rot wages."

"I'll have self-respect!"

"You?" He laughs even louder. "You stood on Boy Street, two nights in a row! You lost your self-respect long ago."

If he knew my mother, then he would know exactly how long ago. Good thing this isn't *Rebel State*, where honor matters.

I bend over my food and mutter, "I can work for you."

"Fine! You can meet a client tonight."

Before Han can stop me, I grab the bottle and chug down some wine.

———

Back at the Church Street coffee bar, the cashier remembers me. I recognize the geometric designs tattooed in blazing colors on her arms.

"Where's your laptop?" she asks, smiling.

I am so surprised that she repeats herself.

"Got stolen," I tell her.

"No!" Her eyes widen. "Where?"

"At the hostel."

She tells me to check the bulletin board. Sometimes people have laptops to sell at low prices.

This place is going to be my hangout. I take my drink to a tall stool at the counter that runs along the wall-sized front window. The street trees are bare of leaves;

their trunks and branches are skeletons. It's chilly but people stroll by without rushing. It's sunny, so sunglasses are bobbing everywhere. Patio chairs and tables sit on the sidewalk, and two hardy souls in sheepskin coats sip their coffee outside. Every now and then, someone walks by and greets them.

Two men saunter by in leather pants and leather jackets, black and shiny. They hold hands and laugh through thick beards. A man hurries by with two dogs, each with a rainbow collar at the neck. They get stopped by a little blonde girl who reaches out to pet them. Before she can do so, a man grabs her hand. He pushes his face close to hers. She looks down at her feet as he scolds her. Her father, I guess. Another man joins them with a stroller holding a younger girl. The girls wear identical jackets. The girls have two fathers. They chat with the dog owner briefly.

Asian men walk by. Were any of them at Rainbow Sushi yesterday? No. Our gazes cross for a second. No telling if they're immigrants or Canadian-born, or if we share a common tongue. In the gay newspaper, raunchy personal ads sit beside those from respectable banks and dentists. I check for events by the Chinese gays. None, but I spot an announcement from a club for on-line game players who are gay.

Maybe I can make new friends there.

Very late that night, Han drives me to my destination.

"This'll be easy," he tells me. "You won't have to do much. Are you scared?"

"If I were, would I be here?"

"Don't worry," he says grandly. "I've known Bruce for many years."

"I'm not afraid," I declare. All the same, I wish I had my cell with me.

"Remember, make small talk with the guest," says Han. "And don't worry about your English. This man, he wants to be your close friend."

The car stops in front of a tall downtown condo near the waterfront. The entrance is glass and marble, with statues of Greek gods standing on high pedestals. They carry spears and raise bows and arrows, ready to fire.

Han phones up to open the door, and then he waves goodbye. By the elevators, a stone fountain spews water from a lion's mouth.

My throat is dry as paper. The elevator is lined with dark wood and brass. High in a corner, a camera watches me.

At a door, Bruce waits with a glass of red wine. He is middle-aged, short and a bit overweight. Strands of long gray hair are pasted over a bald head; a soft belly flops over his belt like a cushion. Jazz music plays in the background.

This man could be anyone: teacher, bank manager, symphony conductor. I can't tell. Nothing in his place reveals much, except that he is well-to-do. Large paintings of cold winter landscapes hang on his walls. His aquarium is as big as a desk, and tropical fish of all colors and sizes glide and twist under a long lamp. A motor hums softly, sending a steady chimney of bubbles to the surface. The water looks very peaceful.

"Do you speak English?" Bruce drops onto a black suede sofa and invites me to sit.

"Yes." I stay standing. "I practice everywhere I go."

"Great. You sound fine. Wayne told me your English was good."

Wayne? That must be Han's English name.

"Are you from China?" he asks.

I nod.

"Shanghai?"

"No, Beijing."

"I've been to China several times," he says. "It's a wonderful place. So much to see, so much history."

"Did you go by yourself? Or with a tour group?"

It's easier to talk than I thought it would be. I guess I know how to go after good tips, too.

"I've tried both ways," he tells me.

I imagine he used money boys every night on his trip. A blessing for China's economy.

"Which do you think is better?" I ask.

"Tour groups. But I'm lucky. I had really good guides, people who spoke good English."

He waves at a bowl of nuts on the coffee table.

"Won't you sit down? I can get you something to drink. Juice? Soft drink?"

I shake my head, wanting to get through this as fast as possible. Out the window and far away, a serpent of bright lights crawls along the freeway.

"Wayne is a good buddy of mine," Bruce says, pouring himself more wine. "We've known each other for years. He said you're a personal friend of his."

"He has been a big help to me," I say.

"Did you meet him here, or in China?"

"Here."

"And you? Do you travel to China much?"

"No, I like it here," I say. My words are a big surprise to me.

Suddenly I want to say new things, think different thoughts. Maybe I shouldn't rush the customer. Maybe we should go slowly. Maybe if we keep talking, Bruce will get distracted and decide not to touch me.

"There is more freedom here," I say, "and the air we breathe is much cleaner. Gay people can get married here. Are you married?"

Bruce winks at me. "Who would want a dumpy old guy like me?"

"Someone who likes tropical fish?"

He chuckles. "I really wanted a dog, but the condo doesn't allow it."

"Some dogs are small as cats."

"Even cats aren't allowed."

He finishes his wine and smiles at me. I freeze. I can't think of anything else to say.

He takes me to a bathroom and tells me to take a shower. The jazz music follows me everywhere. The bathroom is as big as an apartment in China. The shower has so much space that no curtains or glass doors are needed. Its tiles are familiar shades of bamboo: dark and pale greens, yellows and browns. When I turn on the water, streams of water shoot out from spouts high and low. I sniff the soaps and shampoos on the rack. They are sharp and perfumed.

Suddenly Bruce calls out, "Scrub yourself clean, really clean, you hear?"

I spin around. How long has he been there, watching me?

He is wearing a bathrobe now. It is brown. I start to shake, so I make the water hotter. I wait for him, but he seems to want to watch. He has a far-off look in his eyes.

Maybe he's on drugs.

Even if he is dangerous, I'm sure I'm stronger than him. I start to scrub myself again, from top to bottom.

Then, as I shampoo my hair, he starts touching me. He runs his fingers along my back. His arms encircle me from behind and pull me tight against him. He's still wearing his bathrobe. My body tenses. He presses his face against my ear and neck. His beard stubble feels like sandpaper.

I close my eyes and bring Lawrence's face into my mind.

––––––––

The elevator cannot come fast enough. I jump in and bang for the Lobby. I turn away from the camera, wanting to throw up. The car drops only one or two floors before stopping. I straighten up, act as if all is normal.

A young man rushes in. He's a westerner who looks very young, very rich. On his feet are polished black boots, so he's likely going out to party. He wears a black jacket and a black shirt open at the neck where two gold chains hang. I smell perfume.

"Hey, man, how's it going?" His words are slurred. He's been drinking already.

He presses Parking, the doors close, and the elevator drops.

Then he swears and slams a fist on Stop. The elevator bounces to a sudden halt. The doors open.

"Sorry about that." He steps out to wait for an elevator going up.

When the doors close, I throw up. I bend over to avoid soiling myself. I try to catch the slop in my hands but there's too much. I ate several slices of pizza before meeting Han. I thought food would settle my stomach. And I drank two Cokes. Now I let it all drip to the floor in the corner. I stick my hands behind my back. I can't wipe them on my pants. They'll stink.

If the elevator stops and someone steps in, I'll dash out, head down. I'll find the stairs for escaping fires.

Luckily the elevator reaches the lobby without stopping. Luckily there's the fountain. I hold my hands under the lion's mouth for clean water.

The lobby clock says 1:00 a.m. I step outside and start to hail a cab but a car honks at me. A second later, Han pulls up.

At first I'm glad to see him. If only he'd pull me into his arms and hold me tight. I'm trembling all over, but no one can see.

"All washed and clean now?" He sounds cheerful.

He must know what Bruce does. He can't know what happened in the elevator.

"You told me to go home by myself," I remind him.

He treats me like a child.

He holds out one hand and I slap the money into it.

"Don't you trust me?" I demand.

He hands me two bills.

"Is that all?" I say.

"Other nights, you'll get more than one job." He looks around and checks his mirrors. "My other workers have other jobs."

Before he can change gears, I jump from the car and run off.

The bills are crumpled in my hands. Two blocks away, I stop and lean my head against a streetlamp. I'm panting but a choked sob leaks out of me. I want to rip the money into little bits and fling them away. But I can't.

The route to the hostel takes me through club land. On Saturday night, the streets are buzzing. Line-ups of people wait to enter boom-box bars. The throbbing bass shakes my bones. I stop under loudspeakers, wanting the music to drown out all thought. Around me are short, short skirts, long, long legs and clouds of cigarette smoke. I swim through an ocean of aftershave. Party-goers laugh and pose and giggle. Some look and sound like kids from my school.

At the hostel, I use all my strength to brush my teeth and spit out, over and over. If I had mouthwash, I'd swallow the whole bottle.

In my bare feet, I stroll up and down the long hallway. If I lie down, my brain starts racing. The last thing I want now is to think or remember. If the thief who stole my laptop could break into my skull and steal the last sixty minutes of my life, I would pay him well. When I shut my eyes, I see myself lying at the bottom of Bruce's aquarium with my eyes wide open and bulging like those of a fish.

I think of Han. I enjoyed our time together that first night. I wanted to be cool and confident like him. I needed him to show me how men touched one another. I used him. Well, he used me, too, but he paid for it.

When I finally doze off, I am chasing the slave convoy across a snowy plain. My horse suddenly bursts through a huge glass window that springs up from nowhere. Both of us are badly cut, but blood sprays out of the horse like water from a fire hydrant. I have to cut the poor beast's throat by myself. Sobbing and howling, I find my face soaked with sweat and tears and blood. When I run one hand across my cheek, the gory mixture fills my mouth.

That's when I wake up, choking and spitting.

Twelve

In the morning, I stay in bed with my head under the pillow and let the roommates leave. They are new faces, big and blond, and loudly speak a foreign language. German, I think, or Dutch or Russian.

Who cares?

I drag myself downstairs at the last minute, just before the pancake service ends. I force myself to chew and swallow the puffy dough. The orange juice is made from powder. The jug sat out all morning and is warm now. At the same time, the pot of coffee has gotten cold. I can barely drink it, even after adding six spoons of sugar.

The downtown streets are quiet and bleak. It's Sunday. I go to the Internet café to use up my last hour. I'm the only customer there.

I don't log onto *Rebel State*.

Something has changed. I don't want to play this game

anymore. I surf through new Chinese games, looking for another home. There are previews for *Chase Thunder and Mist*, *Mongol Invasion*, *Tai-shan: The Sacred Mountain* and *Yin-Yang Secrets*. I want something different, but the graphics and role sketches from one site to another all look and sound the same. More orphans. More warriors sick of bloodshed. More wanderers fighting for their family's honor.

Maybe it's time for me to play English-language games. That would be a real challenge.

———

The video store on Church Street rents portable DVD players and sells popcorn and coffee. You can park yourself on an easy chair and watch your rentals right in the shop. The Foreign Film section carries all the latest gay movies from China but I choose a Hollywood film about a gay man who gets elected to high public office in San Francisco.

It's an okay movie. I understood most of it. Without Chinese subtitles, I'll need to watch it a few more times to get all the dialogue.

At the main library, I get a half hour of computer time. I log onto Facebook to check up on my old friends.

To my surprise, they're all wondering about me. Jian told everyone that I went to visit a sick relative, but nobody believes him because they haven't heard from me. Mila suspects Niang killed me and buried my body in the backyard. I laugh out loud. Kai thinks Ma has called me home. Wei thinks I'm gambling in Las Vegas. Jenny wonders if someone should report my disappearance to the police.

Have only seven days passed since I got kicked out? Seven thousand things have happened. I'll just tell them the good news: I'm out, I'm not a virgin anymore, and I've made lots of new friends.

But, at the keyboard, my fingers freeze. I'm not ready to post yet. Maybe I need to figure out the best words to use. Chinese terms can be tricky. Maybe I'll write everything down first. This is big news. I want to get it right.

At the hostel, Han has left a telephone message.

Urgent, it says. *Call me.*

No doubt he has a job for me tonight. My throat tightens. I can taste the sour throw-up. I'd rather go back to school than face another Bruce.

I push through the crowd of people waiting to check in. Then a voice calls my name from across the lobby.

It's Ba.

I point to the phone and keep on going.

"I have to talk to someone," I call over the din of the guests.

"Get over here!" he barks. "I'm your father!"

Travelers turn and look curiously at us.

Chen must have sent him here.

In the breakfast room, a woman with long red hair is curled up in an easy chair in one corner, reading a book.

Ba sits at the big table. I walk around it to face him. He pulls out a bag and shoves it over to me. A net-book.

"I meant to give you one, too," he says. "You can come home now."

I push the net-book back across the table.

Ba grabs my arm.

"Come home, I said!" Then he sees the woman in the corner and lowers his voice. "You've been away long enough."

"Let go."

"You are wasting your life out here. What do you want? Tell me!"

He has never asked me that. My mind goes blank for a second.

"Don't order me around," I say. "Stop telling me who I should be."

"Your grandfather is arriving tonight," he says. "I am going to the airport to get him."

I knew it! Ba didn't come here for me. No, he's here to make himself look perfect.

"Come home to welcome him," Ba says.

"No."

"You and your grandfather were always close. You are the only grandson who carries his name."

The wall behind Ba holds a huge map of the world. China's bulge and Canada's rectangle are different shades of pink. A wide blue ocean separates and connects them. Beijing is thirteen hours ahead of Toronto. An airplane takes fourteen hours to fly between the two cities.

"Your grandfather lived a difficult life," Ba adds. "For many years, the nation starved. His health is not good. Son, this..." His voice falters. "This may be your last chance to see him."

So soon? Then, I remember. Grandfather is over seventy years old. He smoked all his life, too.

"Is he really coming?" I ask.

Ba nods. "He is on the airplane now. Before he boarded, he phoned to make sure you would be at home."

I look at the pink slip with Han's message on it.

Urgent, it says.

Where do I want to be tonight?

———

I open the drawers, one after another, and press my nose into my clothes. Every T-shirt and sweatshirt is present. Everything is freshly laundered. Stepmother must have sent my clothes through the washing machine after they were rescued from outside. I wonder who got that job.

Ba? Jian? Or Stepmother herself? Did they have a big fight over it?

The first thing I do is to catch up with my friends. I log onto the desktop. As it warms up, I think of what to say. I use the dictionary. My friends will be surprised to get an English email from me.

Today I came home because Grandfather is visiting. My father evicted me last week. He learned I'm gay. I went downtown and saw more of this world. I am glad to tell you this. See you at school tomorrow.

I hit the Send button before I can change my mind.

I don't want to be scared anymore. I don't want to be afraid of being gay. That would be as cowardly as saying, "I'm not Chinese" just so I could fit into Canada.

Ba, Stepmother and Jian went to the airport to fetch Grandfather. I'm supposed to clean myself up.

In the basement, I jack up the music and give my old friend the weight machine a solid kick. I do bench presses for chest and shoulders. I do rowing for the back, extensions and raises for the legs. The pain and tightness feel good. I want to stay fit. Maybe I can do gymnastics again.

After the hottest shower in many days, I lie down. The bed feels like it is part of my body.

———

The persistent dinging of the doorbell wakes me.

How long was I napping?

It's dark outside. I stumble to the front door.

It's Carla. I didn't send her my email.

"Jian's not home," I tell her.

"I came to see you."

She walks in but doesn't take off her jacket. Her arms are wrapped around her. Her face is pinched, as if she's cold. She keeps looking at the ground.

"We saw you on Thursday," she says in her bad Mandarin. "At the shelter. Jian went looking for you but you were gone. This morning, when Jian told me you were gay, I knew that you ran from us because you saw me. That's not right. That shelter is there because God wants us to help people."

"Jian's a good guy," I say. "I didn't want to make trouble between you and him."

"I'm glad you're home," she says. "Family is important."

She hugs me, and I smell the lemon shampoo in her hair again. She turns to leave but there are people at the back door. Ba is shouting at someone to be careful, to walk slowly. Niang is telling Ba not to push.

Grandfather's ears still stick out, and his eyeglasses are thicker than ever. His eyes are alert but he has shrunk like a dried apple. The white whiskers on his face are longer. He stabs the floor with a cane as his feet shuffle along. He doesn't have the strength to lift them anymore. And he wears his Mao jacket and Chinese army cap, as usual, with a thick scarf wrapped around his neck.

He has lost two of his front teeth. The last time we saw each other, we were about the same height. Now I tower like a giant above him.

The shock chills me to my bones. Do all old people shrink like this?

Grandfather calls eagerly to me, but Ba moves him through to the living room to sit down. Grandfather insists that Ba fetch him a sturdy chair, nothing too soft. He reaches out with both hands and seizes my hands. His grip is strong and warm. He smells of Chinese medicinal oil.

"You have grown," he says. "You remind me of my father. He was big, taller than me. I was the runt in the family."

I kneel and press my face into his arm, letting his sleeve soak up my tears. Inside my chest, I'm clenching a loud sob that I can't let out in front of everyone.

I didn't know that I missed him so much. I never thought about all the time Grandfather put into my life. I'm glad we'll have time together. I'll do anything to make him happy.

When Jian pushes Carla forward, Grandfather looks

at me and exclaims, "She is beautiful! Is she your girl-friend?"

"No, Grandfather," I reply. "Ba set a rule that Jian and I cannot have girlfriends until we finish college. She is a classmate. She came over to study."

"But, Rui-yong, your abilities are just average!" Grandfather cries. "By the time you finish college, you will be an old man like me. No girl will want you!"

Everyone laughs, including me.

"Sit, Rui-yong, sit. It has taken me so long to make this visit because this old man was afraid to get on an airplane. But I wanted to see you, one last time."

"I wanted to see you, too, Grandfather," I say. "Ba said I could go home during the summer if my marks were high enough. But they never were."

"He has to study harder!" Ba calls out.

"I was never good at school, either," Grandfather says to me. "Maybe it is too much to hope for, to see you go to college."

"I have a part-time job at a Japanese restaurant. Maybe I'll become a sushi chef," I say, looking at Ba.

He doesn't say anything. Neither does Niang. On our way home, I told Ba that I would go back to school only if I could stop working for Niang and start at Rainbow Sushi instead.

Ba turns to his father and says, "Tell the boy he still

needs to study. Tell him not to let the cooked duck fly away! Tell him — "

Niang steps in. "Grandfather, in Canada there are many ways to make a good living. It is not like China."

Then the kettle whistle calls her to the kitchen.

"Working with your hands is respectable, too. Look how we admire artists," Grandfather says. "Even if he does not go to college, he can give me a great-grand-child with my surname. That is more important than a degree."

Niang calls from the kitchen, "Rui-yong, come take the tea out."

She's trying to rescue me but I don't move.

"No man in our family ever lived long enough to see the fourth generation," Grandfather continues. "Now people are living longer."

Niang hurries out with a clatter of teapot and cups. Smoothly, she steps in front of me.

"Try this Dragon Well tea, Grandfather," she says. "A friend just brought this from China. She says the quality is very high."

"Rui-yong, will you let me embrace a great-grand-child one day?" Grandfather leans to one side to peer at me. His lips are quivering.

I pause.

"Say yes," Ba whispers. He is standing right behind me.

"Grandfather, I can't," I blurt. "I'm a homosexual."

The room is deathly quiet for a second. Nobody breathes. We all stare at Grandfather. He sits like a statue.

Ba curses me under his breath and then tells Grandfather, "Do not listen to him. He is talking nonsense."

"Hush," Niang says. "Let the two of them talk. This is none of your business!"

"In Canada, this is not a problem," Jian quickly tells Grandfather.

"Homosexual?" Grandfather speaks the word carefully as if saying it for the first time ever. He looks at me. "Are you sure? Do you know what you are saying?"

I take a deep breath. "Yes, Grandfather. Absolutely sure."

He frowns, and deep furrows cut into his forehead. He opens his mouth, but a coughing fit seizes him. It's a dry hacking that comes from deep inside him. It goes on and on, scaring me. Niang puts her hand on his shoulder, but he waves her away.

Finally he recovers.

"But this is Canada," he says hoarsely. "Homosexuals are allowed to marry, is that not so? That is the law here, is it not?"

I swallow hard before I can speak and make things clear.

"Yes. But I won't be marrying a woman."

"So adopt a child, or make a baby through test tubes!" Grandpa exclaims. "I read about it in the newspapers."

I stammer, "I haven't thought of children."

"Ah, you are too young. Your entire life lies ahead of you." He's smiling.

I close my eyes and let his words sink in. My shoulders loosen, and a rush of warmth fills me.

Then Grandfather looks around. He thumps his cane, and his voice booms out, as strong as it used to be.

"Where is my tea? Is it still hot?"